A WEATHER GIRL'S GUIDE TO LOVE

BY

CASSANDRA JOELLE

cassandrajoelle.com
ISBN: 979-8-9910488-4-2

For my husband-
My real-life cowboy and the sweetest surprise
in my Wyoming forecast.

TABLE OF CONTENTS

CHAPTER 1:
STORM FRONT INCOMING

The campus news makeup artist is either going into the mortuary field or special effects makeup, I thought to myself as I looked at my reflection. I didn't know it was legal to be wearing this many layers of makeup before sundown.

"What do you think, girlie?" As Breanna held the mirror and smiled at me expectantly, I didn't want to discourage her or make any abrupt facial expressions, as the whole facade of powder may come tumbling down.

"Thank you, Breanna. I appreciate you doing my makeup for my final weather presentation. I can't believe I'm graduating tomorrow." Aversion did the trick, and she happily took the mirror and started cleaning her brushes.

I took the hallway to the campus television station, stopping by the ladies room to dab, buff, or wipe whatever excesses I could away, but not surprisingly, she must have used a waterproof formula because it just wouldn't budge. I went ahead and removed both rows of false lashes and the dark lipliner and was able to soften my blush slightly, which made me look more my age. It was as good as it could get when I made it to my presentation.

The cameraman was new on set, and I didn't have time to introduce myself nor speak to anyone before his camera honed in on my green screen, prompting a quick start to the broadcast. I stood up straight, smiled, and did what I loved to do.

"Hailey Sinclair coming to you from Northwoods University with today's weather report! It's a gorgeous day here in Northwood, with clear skies and an unusually warm high of 73 degrees—practically summer by May standards. But don't pack away your winter coat just yet! A strong cold front is barreling down from Canada, bringing gusty winds and a sharp drop in temperatures by tomorrow. We're still in a La Niña pattern, and while this winter has been deceptively calm, meteorologists predict a strong moisture event on the horizon. Enjoy the clear skies while they last!" I stood on my platform, as I knew the green screen behind me would be changing from weather icons to my school's logo, and waited for the cameraman to signal we were off air. As it appeared the new cameraman was struggling to turn off the recording, I sat a moment longer than normal mulling on my final words. Was that choice of phrase. . .ominous? The stage manager finally came over and helped him shut off the camera. Stepping off the stage, the school newsroom teacher, Mrs. Jackson, came over with her notorious clipboard that I'd never seen her without.

"Great job as usual, Hailey." She reached in for a hug. "I can't believe this is it. I don't know who we will find next year. They will have big shoes to fill."

I released from our embrace and thanked her.

"You've been a great teacher, coach, and friend to me these last few years. I've learned so much from this program, and your guidance. Thanks to you, Mrs. Jackson, I feel confident about my future. I'll never forget you, and I promise to keep in touch."

She looked teary-eyed in response to my words and took a moment to gather herself as she started flipping through her stack of papers.

"There's something I've been waiting to give you. Here."

She handed me a manilla envelope. I turned it over and undid the clasp, pulling out a stack of beautifully typeset letters. Skimming the documents, I saw they were all professional recommendation letters to future employers.

"It's been years since I've seen such a passion for meteorology like I do in you. Your dreams will be attained. I can feel it in my bones that I am going to see you on television one day, Hailey. And I bet it will be sooner than we think."

My heart caught fire at her belief in me, and I said a silent prayer that my dreams would be realized.

That afternoon, I gathered up the last of my things in my small, off-campus apartment. After this weekend, I'd be off to my new apartment in Chicago, where Jett would follow shortly thereafter. I found a darling studio apartment that was the perfect amount of space to start out with, while Jett planned on living with a roommate, organized by his school. While I had already paid the first, last and security deposit, the clock would be ticking for me to secure employment as fast as possible. But in a city that large, I felt luck was on my side. As I packed, I replayed my future in my head. I had it all planned out, to a perfect *T*. It was so perfect, in fact, books would be written about it. *"The Girl Who Made Only Good Choices."*

I bent down to check under the bed and spotted a familiar shoebox. Not just any shoebox—the shoebox. The one that held my childhood dreams. I lifted the lid and smiled. Inside was a weather scrapbook I made in third grade, bursting with cloud formations, facts from science magazines, and clippings of Dana Summers, the queen of meteorology and my childhood hero. The next day, I would graduate with my degree in meteorology.

I spent every evening watching Dana Summers give the weather reports on the KA News. Her hair was blonde, curly, and larger than life, just like mine and my late mother's hair. She wore flashy jewelry, sky high heels, and had long, brightly painted nails. Her outfits were high end, made out of thick, luxurious fabrics that you'd only find in a department store. I could have used some help in that area, but surely by the time I became a national weather girl, there would have been wardrobes and professional manicurists at my beck and call. And that's what I was going to become: a weather forecaster for a big-time news network. One that my friends, relatives, acquaintances, and everyone who had ever met me would see if they tuned in to a big channel.

I would finally move out of suburbia and into the big city, where everyone would know me. My life would be glamorous as I lived in an upper floor apartment in a high rise. My news network would have me fill in on other projects where I'd get the chance to travel the world exploring weather patterns, storm tracking, and post-disaster aid. I thought the parts I most looked forward to was helping people in some way; bringing awareness to those in need, sharing my faith with those down and out.

By then, my last name would surely be changed to Dawson, because the man of my dreams, Jett Dawson would have proposed, and our elopement would have commenced shortly thereafter. He was the perfect man for me; tall to my petite, slightly darker shade of blonde, which would almost guarantee we would procure an army of blonde Barbie and Ken children. Our plans fit perfectly together because he was graduating the next day also, which made me study harder and faster so that I could at the same time. He planned on taking a few weeks off before going into law school, which worked perfectly with my plans, as he would be relocating to Chicago to do so; therefore, I set my sights on all major new networks that operated there.

Jett never had much to say about those plans; he was a man of few words, which sometimes frustrated me. I had always been incredibly driven and liked a well-laid plan. As my mother always said, "If you fail to plan, you plan to fail." I wholeheartedly lived my life that way.

We grew up only a state away from each other but lived dramatically different lives. He was a country boy, living in rural Wyoming—while I lived in a lively, bustling city (a term generously applied to anywhere in Montana), but still much larger in comparison. We met at Freshman orientation, and I took one look at him and knew he fit into my perfect plan. Thankfully, we hit it off, and he asked me to be his girlfriend a week later. His parents came out that year for Easter weekend, and my father along with his wife and children came too, and it was an instant connection. Everyone hit it off that weekend, especially me with his mother. Jett and Cindy were very close, something that I really appreciated, as she gave her blessing for our relationship from the get go. I never felt anything except love from her, which I considered an honor as she approved of me dating her one and only beloved child. Cindy and I had become very close during the three-year relationship with Jett, and for that, I was very thankful, as my mother passed when I was a child.

Jett and I had a very quiet relationship. We saw each other at lunch and dinner once or twice a week, and we attended church on Sundays. While there was always a yearning for more time spent, I knew marriage was just around the corner for us, and I looked forward to that time in my life.

But for then, we'd both been swimming upstream as he prepared for law school, and I was working to become a national news figure. I closed the scrapbook, put it back in its shoebox, and packed it with the rest of my things.

My phone buzzed, slapping me out of my daydream. Jett Dawson's name flashed across the screen. "Hello, darling," I said in my best British accent. Jett wasn't the silly type, and I knew that, but usually I would get a small chuckle in response. This time, his voice was purely professional.

"Hailey, can I take you to dinner tonight, instead of tomorrow?" The sudden switch threw me off. We'd been planning that dinner for months. And I secretly hoped it would be the following day that we would be taking the next step in our relationship, i.e., engagement. His cancelling of said dinner and moving it abruptly to that night threw me off. As he asked, I looked at the clock, expecting it to already be far too late to eat a meal; therefore, he would have to take me the next day as planned. But alas, it was only half past 3, and I agreed.

"Sure, that should work." I gave him space to respond with a platitude of thanks, or an explanation, but when he was silent, I spoke again. "Is everything alright?" He made a long winded sigh that I could only describe as an audible disappointment, before promising to explain everything that night at dinner.

My thoughts went from joyous to concern in a matter of seconds. As he ended the call as abruptly as it began, I shuffled to my closet. I had planned on wearing the dress I would graduate in for our nice dinner, so I needed to find something else. I assumed we would still be going to our favorite Italian restaurant, so I slipped into a black shift dress and a black cardigan sweater with white trim on top, paired with a pair of black high heels. It felt elegant as I topped it off with pearl earrings. I tried to dress every day like it was a job interview for a television network, including dates with Jett and Sundays at church. As I gave myself a glance in the mirror, I repeated my favorite phrase that Dana Summers said after every weather forecast, "Rain or shine—see you next time," while practicing my perfect television smile.

Dana Summers became a motherly figure to me after my mom died when I was seven. Since my mother was a hairstylist, I used to go to sleep pretending that she hadn't passed away, but that she was off touching up the roots on Dana's perfect hair. When she'd get back, she would tell me all of Dana's secrets, like what nail polish color was her favorite. What her shoe size was. Or what perfume she wore. My mother would surely be back any minute, and the cancer that she had would be miraculously cured. I couldn't wait to hear how Dana smelled like amber and smoked Virginia Slims while driving a red corvette. She would surely know it all, and I would lap up the information like a housecat with fresh milk.

My dad didn't know what to do with me once she passed, understandably. I never blamed him for that; my mother was the one raising me. A relative of my mother saw the situation we were in and offered for me to come stay there for the summer with her in Oregon. My father obliged; we both knew that it was for the best. I learned about Natalie, my mother's second cousin, who had a small two-bedroom house and no family of her own. When I first arrived at the airport in Oregon, fresh with grief, Natalie was standing at the gate.

"You must be Hailey." There was a glamour to Natalie that I found comforting. She wasn't on the scale of glamour that Dana Summers was of course, but she was certainly more than I expected to find in Oregon. My father had told me that this was a state of beautiful scenery, greenery and horses. But where Natalie lived sure felt more like a city than anywhere else. Even back home in Montana, we were a little ways from town. For the first time, I got a taste of life outside of my world.

The only home I'd ever known. My crippling grief that I didn't understand.

I returned and spent two more summers with Natalie before I moved in with her full time. As it turned out, there was a high school internship for a meteorologist in Oregon and with my father's blessing and Natalie's generosity, the move made sense for my future. My father had remarried by then, so me leaving was like the last of the memories of my mother leaving with me, and though we never said it out loud, I think there was some relief there.

Once dressed, I sat on my bed, since it was the only furniture I had that wasn't draped with sheets after I shampooed them. All of the furniture stayed with this apartment. I had about an hour left until Jett picked me up, so I started scrolling some funny memes and instinctively sent them to his mother, Cindy. She and I texted a few times a day and spoke at least once a week, so when I hadn't gotten a response from her after a few moments, I gave her a call. Listening to the ringing go on and on, I assumed she was out at the movies with a friend or had her hands busy kneading a loaf of bread, so I left a message.

"Hello my favorite! You must be out having fun. Or are you giving yourself a pedicure and have your toes in those foam separators and can't waddle to the phone in time? Anyway, going to see your darling son tonight. Hope all is well, love you!"

The sentiment was so real. Sometimes I would tease Jett that I loved his mother more than him. He was never bothered by this, and in fact, he agreed. His mother had gone above and beyond for him, me, and everyone she ever met. She was the true meaning of a Christian, sharing Christ-like love with anyone in her path.

Checking the time, the hour had passed quickly, and any moment, Jett would be there. Just then, he knocked on the door. I opened it quickly, smiling ear to ear, but my expression fell when I saw the look on his face.

"Jett? What's wrong?" I gave him a hug, as it looked like he needed one. He accepted, but didn't return the gesture.

"I'm sorry, Hailey. My mind is in another world today. I'll explain it at dinner. Are you ready? I'm starved."

"Oh—okay." I robotically reached for my purse from where I hung it on the doorknob earlier, slid my phone inside, and locked the door behind me.

The car ride to the restaurant was silent. I peeked over at Jett, wondering what on earth had him in that place. Did his law school retract his admission? Did he uncover something disturbing about his future roommate? Did he . . .Want to break up with me? My stomach flipped at the last one, but I couldn't assume everything was about me. It would explain the hug gesture, but I would wait to see what he had to say first.

After getting to the restaurant, he quickly jumped out of the car, swiftly opening my side for me like the gentleman he was. We walked in holding hands as usual, so the thoughts of us breaking up left my mind, but Iwas greatly worried for what was to come.

As the waiter came by with the menus, we waived them off, both already knowing what we were going to get. I ordered the chicken parmesan, and Jett the lasagna with an extra piece of garlic bread, and a bottle of Acqua Panna, our favorite water. As soon as the waiter turned around and left, I looked at Jett, expectantly. He nodded, taking a deep breath.

"My mom has stage 4 pancreatic cancer. I'll be returning home tomorrow right after graduation to take care of her—however long it takes." My jaw dropped to the floor. The woman I loved like my own mother, was experiencing a health crisis similar to my mother. I couldn't believe it. I was so tired of cancer.

"I'll come with you, Jett. I love her like my own mother." Jett's eyes brightened for a moment before he shook his head.

"No, Hailey. I can't ask you to do that. You'd be putting off your dreams. You already have an apartment on deposit." I thought about going to Chicago one more time before finalizing my decision, but it was already made the moment I heard the news.

"I want to come. I would do anything for Cindy. And having been through this before, I know what it's like. I can help with things. I want to be there for her, and for you." I reached out for his hand, but the waiter dropped off our water, and I put my hand back on my lap. "I'm so sorry, Jett. God is bigger than this. I promise I will be praying every moment of the day for her."

"Thank you," was all Jett could mumble before our food swiftly came, and he immediately dug in. I noticed then that his blue eyes and tan skin looked red and blotchy from crying. I felt my own tears coming on, but I would be strong for Jett.

A storm was coming. I just didn't realize I was standing in the eye of it.

CHAPTER 2:
CLOUDY WITH A CHANCE OF CRINGE

Turned out, cancelling an apartment deposit in a big city came with a few headaches. For one, I wouldn't be getting my $2,100 deposit back. For the last five years, I'd been saving every penny I could from my job at a business clothing boutique for that move, so that hurt. And the other whammy? The landlords had a list of tenants a mile long, so my best chance of getting that perfect, dreamy apartment in Chicago wouldn't happen for another two years at minimum. When my thoughts returned to Cindy and her diagnosis, I felt guilty as heck. "Lord, I'm sorry for being so selfish. Cindy is more important to my life than any silly apartment. Please work this out for the good of your glory."

Next on the agenda was finding a place to live in Wyoming. I knew Jett was from a small town, but I didn't know just how small until I tried to look up a rental company online.

While there wasn't a formal business who professionally rented out places, there was a real estate company, so I gave them a ring to see if they had any leads.

"This is Sharon."

I always got confused when people answered the phone this way. What was I supposed to say? "This is Hailey"? And then we go back and forth making statements in the third person?

"Hi, Sharon. My name is Hailey, and I am looking for a place to live in your town, and I was wondering if you could give me some leads."

The first questions she asked threw me off the carousel.

"Sure, Hailey. How soon will you be here? And how long of a lease are you looking for?" I considered the questions for the first time.

"I need to be there as soon as possible, as my lease is ending in two days, and I'll start with six months to be safe, but may need to transition into something longer." As I said the words aloud, Cindy's diagnosis hit me like a punch to the gut. I very much hoped she would be with us for as long as possible. The pain formed a lump in my throat, and I felt like I was fighting off tears.

"I have just the place for you, Hailey. There's a small, one-bedroom home that just came up for rent. It's $700 a month, no pets or smoking. It's got a tiny porch, a tiny backyard, and it's a block off Main Street, so you could walk pretty much anywhere. Give me your email address, and I can send you the details and pictures."

The relief washed over me like water, and I thanked her profusely and asked for the application along with it. I couldn't imagine it would be bad enough that I would turn it down, as the alternative of not going was much worse.

The pictures weren't great, but the place seemed fine. It looked old, outdated, but very clean. There were even a few pieces of furniture that appeared to be included. Looking up the home on Google Maps, I want to see what the neighborhood was like. In the photos of the home and the neighbors' homes, there were several roosters in each yard. I didn't know a thing about birds, and certainly didn't pretend to, so I quickly submitted my application and sent it back Sharon's way.

My email chimed less than five minutes later with an approval, contingent on the first and last month's rent and another hefty deposit. I checked my bank balance, and according to my miserly balance, I had exactly enough plus an extra few hundred dollars to get me going on utilities. I said a short prayer under my breath. I knew this was what was right; time with Cindy was worth more to me than my dreams of Chicago. I just prayed I could find a job the day I arrived.

On that note, I started browsing online for job listings. It looked like Wyoming had plenty of opportunities in fields I knew nothing about, like gun manufacturing and energy. I clicked on a job posting titled, "The Beef Boss," just to find out it was for a jerky maker at a processing plant. While I enjoyed beef jerky now and then, I had an inclination that it was not something I'd enjoy doing. "Lord, please guide me to where you want me to work," I said aloud as I continued to scroll. My phone dinged, pulling me away from my computer. It was the reminder I set that it was time to get ready for my graduation ceremony, as if I would have forgotten it under any other circumstances. Though that day, I was glad for the timer.

I had a little pep in my step, as the day was something I worked very hard for, and I excitedly slipped into the dress I had bought last year for the occasion. It was an off-brand knock off of a dress that Dana Summers wore to a network award show one year. It was an A-line black dress with an exposed electric blue zipper running up the entire backside. What really set the look apart was her matching blue bangles and heels. While I couldn't afford to get the entire look, I got similar bracelets and wore my classic, sturdy, reliable black heels. As I put on my cap and gown, I felt a wave of emotion hit me. "You did it," I spoke to my reflection in the mirror, who still felt like the seven-year-old girl waiting all night for the weather segment to repeat over and over. The little girl who would trick herself into falling asleep, despite her grief, because she would be okay one day. That day is had come. I made it. "Rain or shine—." I couldn't finish my sentence before my emotions got to me.

The ceremony was exciting. As I arrived, I didn't see Jett anywhere. We were to be seated alphabetically, so according to my chart, his seat was in the third row, but he was not present. I assumed he was just running late and put the thought out of my mind while I took my seat in the 11th row. While I attended a small college in southern Oregon, I still wasn't expecting as big of an event as they put on. There were giant banners and a beautiful outdoor stage despite the rainy and windy weather. *Wait, when did the weather change?* I asked myself. It was blue skies and calm that morning. I thought back to my forecast from the day before; if only graduation could've happened a day earlier. It had to be the cold front I saw moving in on the radar. I clung to my graduation gown to warm up while I waited to take the stage.

When they called Jett's name, no one stood. They gave it a few moments before moving on to the next name. He missed graduation? That wasn't like him. A twinge of sadness struck in my gut as I considered sending him a message. I battled between wanting to be present in the moment, and present for my boyfriend. I finally pulled out my phone from my gown pocket and sent him a text message.

"At graduation. They just called your name. Are you okay?" By the time I hit send, I'd retyped it a few times and also felt a chill come over me. As soon as I put my phone back in my pocket, I realized my turn to go was coming up quickly.

"Hailey Sinclair." I stood up, attempting to walk gracefully in my heels, but since my body was catching a chill, it was harder. "Hailey is graduating with her degree in Meteorology. She hopes to work at a large news network in Chicago. Congratulations, Hailey."

As I walked the stage, rain drops pricked my face and the wind tugged at my gown. The president of the college shook my hand and handed me my diploma. Somewhere in the crowd, I imagined my mom, beaming proud.

When the ceremony was over, I was standing alone as my classmates were getting swarmed by family and friends.

My phone buzzed, and I reached for it swiftly. It was a text from my dad.

"So proud of you, Hailey. We saw you graduate on the livestream. Your little sister and brother said they can't wait to go to college."

Smiling, I texted him back a message of thanks, appreciation, and to pass along that I said hello to his other children. While I did consider them siblings, I so rarely saw or spoke to the newest members of my family, it almost didn't seem real. And since my mother died, my childhood almost felt like a dream sometimes. I was thrilled that my father remarried and had more children because I knew it made him happy. But we didn't speak that much. In fact, I spoke to Jett's mother more than anyone else, including Jett.

I gave Jett another few minutes before ultimately deciding to leave. Since it was over, I needed to start packing up my SUV and pick up the U-Haul trailer I reserved for the move. I made a quick stop back at my place, taking a selfie in front of my long mirror, considering I didn't get any at the ceremony. I changed into black leggings, a button up shirt, and threw a baggy college sweater on top, and pulled out a white pair of tennis shoes. It felt good to wear soft socks after a cold, blustery day in heels at least.

Once I returned home from U-Haul, I loaded everything into the trailer, checking my phone every half hour or so, expecting to hear from Jett. When all was packed except my bed and the bedding that I would put in my backseat the next day, I made a bag of microwave popcorn and crawled under the covers. I tried calling Jett a few times, but no answer each time. I said a prayer for him before falling asleep.

The drive to Wyoming was a rollercoaster of emotions. I started out feeling groggy, hitting the first coffee hut I came across. Since I planned to do the drive in a straight shot in one day, I knew caffeine was in order, and lots of it. Later, while I was refueling at a gas station in Coeur D'Alene, Idaho, a news van pulled up beside me, and I about lost it, choking back tears and all. "Lord, please take my pain away."

While I found it increasingly odd that I had yet to speak to Jett and hadn't heard a word from him since our dinner two nights earlier, I chalked it up to the spotty cell phone service between Oregon and Wyoming. I pulled into Wyoming around nine at night and met Sharon at the rental property.

"Hailey?" Sharon was a little taller than me, but we had similar larger-than-life curly hair. She reached a hand out. "Sharon from Wild West Realty. So lovely to meet you." She handed me the keys to the rental while chatting me up excitedly about the home, even offering to help get a few boxes inside. "I turned the heat on about an hour ago, and good thing, too. I don't know what is going on with the weather, but it sure is frigid outside."

She was right about that. Just standing out there for a moment, my teeth felt like they were chattering. She led me inside, where the lights were on, too. It felt welcoming, but it was even smaller than the photos looked, yet clean, minus the couch, that was. It looked worn out, deflated and defeated—much similar to how I felt that day.

I took her up on her offer to help unload a few boxes, just what I needed that night, like my bathroom items, kitchen and clothing. The rest of my odds and ends could wait, but truthfully, there wasn't much, and we ended up unloading the whole trailer in about fifteen minutes.

"That took me three hours to load!" I laughed as Sharon dropped the last box in the living room.

"Things always go faster when you have help, don't you think?" She was right about that. "I also have a little housewarming present for you. Here." She picked up a bag from outside the front door. It was a mattress protector. "The mattress is like-new, but not completely new, I'm afraid. Although the only person that's slept on it is my child, I can't guarantee that it's not covered in orange juice and crackers. So, this should protect your sheets from that."

"Thank you so much for your kindness and generosity with helping me move in and providing this. I look forward to staying here."

"Wyoming is lucky to have you. You're going to do big things here, Hailey. I can tell." Sharon smiled and said goodnight, but the moment I shut the door behind her, I wished all of her words to be untrue. This was just a temporary stop on my path to my big dreams, and nothing would get in my way of that.

I didn't sleep well overnight. There were creaks and squeaks, the plumbing sounded questionable, and at one point, I thought the dilapidated couch might be moving. When the neighborhood roosters started screaming at dawn, I gave up trying to rest at all and decided to set up my coffee maker. "Just what I need: surround sound roosters, coming at me from every angle." The kitchen was so small I could almost touch both walls by standing in the middle and reaching my arms out. But once I made a cup of coffee and watched the sunrise, I felt thankful to be there at that time, if anything, for Cindy.

A few hours went by, and I called Jett again. That time, he answered.

"Hey, Hailey. Sorry I went MIA. Drove out here after our dinner the other night and been catching up with my mom." I wasn't surprised in the slightest. I would've done the same for my mom.

"That's okay; I understand. Well, I'm here now, all settled into a rental. Can you give me your address? If it's okay, I'd like to come by today and see you both."

"You're here? In Wyoming? Already?" Jett's voice was the highest I'd ever heard it.

"Uh, yeah. My lease was up in Oregon yesterday. Why do you seem surprised?"

"I guess I forgot; I'm sorry. I just didn't expect it to be so soon. What's your address? I'll come pick you up." I gave him my info, and he said he'd be there within the hour, but twenty minutes went by and as I was laying out an area rug, I heard a knock on the door.

"Welcome to my humble abode." I smiled, giving my best bow and wave so he would come inside, but he still looked like he just put his tongue in an electrical outlet. As he finally stepped inside, cautiously, he turned to me.

"Are you sure about this, Hailey? I can't see you enjoying it here in Wyoming. It's very, very boring." Jett was surely right about that.

"Well, long distance isn't really my forte. Besides, I meant what I said. I really want to be here for you and Cindy. What is the alternative?" Jett went silent, and his expression wasn't great either.

"What? What, Jett? What is it?"

"Nothing." He shook his head, his expression fading and his shoulders sunk. "I'm glad you're here. You're so kind, Hailey. I don't know that I could do this for anyone. Thank you." I wasn't sure how to interpret his words. I was his girlfriend of three years. Was he really that surprised?

"You're welcome. Now, I'd really love to see Cindy if she's feeling up to a visitor?" Jett nodded, his hands on his hips, still looking around my rental in disbelief. "Let me just grab my coat; it's in here somewhere. Give me a moment to find it." I went into my bedroom and started ransacking my clothing boxes when I finally pulled out a black puffer jacket. It was cropped, perfectly stylish for Chicago winters, but might have been perfectly useless out there in frigid Wyoming.

"How long is your lease for?" Jett's voice echoed through the small house, not that he needed to try. I thought I could hear him blink through the paper-thin walls.

"Six months to start. I can extend it as well." I didn't want to put a timeframe on Cindy's life, nor did I want to limit

God and His timing for mine. "I thought we could figure things out after that." Jett didn't respond physically or verbally to the information, but when I slipped on some black boots over my leggings, he opened the door for me, and we left.

The drive to his childhood home was about fifteen minutes down a windy, gusty corridor. Fresh snow could be seen in the hills surrounding and the towering mountain peaks above them. Just on the ride there, I saw horses of all colors, a flock of sheep, and a small herd of elk nestled up. It was beautiful there, despite its lack of everything else.

When we arrived, Jett turned off the ignition but didn't move. He was stalling, but I could tell he wanted to tell me something, so I sat in silence practicing my patience.

"It's progressing pretty fast, I'm afraid. But today is a very good day. You might not realize there's anything going on at all if I hadn't told you otherwise. Part of me wishes I didn't know. She didn't tell me for an entire month. The only reason she did tell me was because the treatments are not working, so she's moved into palliative care."

That was a term I hoped to never hear again. A flashback of my mother in a hospital bed came rushing to me. I braced myself to see Cindy the same way but instead, as we reached the front door, she answered with her radiant smile.

She was wearing a bright blue sweater, and her head was wrapped in a shiny chartreuse scarf that made her blue eyes even brighter. I hugged her as hard as I could and finally, the tears flowed, uncontrollably. It felt joyous to see her, even then , under those circumstances, and her reciprocal tears told me she felt the same.

Jett gave us time to visit alone by telling her he'd go pick up the groceries, and despite her bright face, it was clear her energy was fading fast. We made it to the couch, and she nearly fell back into it.

"It is so good to see you my dear. Thank you for coming. Tell me about graduation. Don't leave anything out." So, I told her all about it, including the details of my outfit, to which she knew just the one. "I remember that award show. Dana Summers did have a very memorable outfit, as usual." And I told her about the drive out there. But just when I started telling her about the rental, she cut me off. "Darling, darling. No. You can't be serious. You're going to Chicago right after this, right? Don't tell me that you're staying here in this ole place to keep an eye on me." She was smiling as she spoke, but I felt a stern tone to her voice that was new to me.

"That's exactly what I'm doing. I'm here for at least six months, maybe more." I took her hand in mine. "You have been like a mother to me, and there's no convincing me otherwise." Cindy smiled, but it didn't reach her eyes. "I have nowhere else I'd rather be."

"Alright then, it's settled. You will be responsible for picking out all of the movies for our family movie night. A tradition that's long been held by myself, and the position as movie picker; I've been waiting to pass that responsibility onto someone else." Cindy gave me a wink and put her arm around me as we sat on the couch. I started rambling off movie titles that I knew she and I would love, and Jett and his father would not, which made her laugh—the sound of which brought me pure joy. When Jett returned from the store, carrying several grocery bags in tow, I got up to help him put them away, and Cindy mentioned she was feeling fatigued and needed to lie down.

"I'll let you sleep, then. I better be going anyway—I have a few things I need to do, but I'll be back every day." I gave Cindy a hug, thinking about my ever-nagging requirement of getting a job so that I could get groceries of my own. Jett hurriedly put away the refrigerated items and threw two pints of mint chip ice cream in the freezer—both Cindy and Jett's favorite flavor—and walked me to the door.

"Be right back, mom," he hollered before shutting the door behind him. On the ride back, Jett barely said anything to me, and I was beginning to see that it was the new normal. Since we were still in a romantic relationship, I tried to give him a kiss when he dropped me off, but it was not reciprocated. I understood he was hurting, but that hurt me a little, too.

"I'm sorry, I just—," he paused, looking out the driver's side window, "not in the mood for this." I nodded, feeling ridiculous that I was just having bad feelings about it and again seeing my selfishness. I was about to tell him that I understood when he started up again. "I didn't think you'd be here for this. Honestly, Hailey—I assumed we'd break up when I didn't go to Chicago, and we'd go our separate ways." His words stunned me like a cattle prod, and I was left breathless.

"What are you getting at, Jett? Were you *hoping* we would break up? Do you not want me here?" I started recounting the scenes in my head of just how I got to be out there. It was a mutual decision, wasn't it?

"I wasn't hoping for anything. I just figured that's what would go down. So, I think I'm mentally prepared for that. Besides, it's not like our relationship has been that great. I'm just a part of your master plan, a steppingstone to get on television. Do you even love me?" Tears welled in my eyes as Jett spoke. I'd never heard him be so cruel before.

"How can you say that? Why are you being so mean? Of course I love you, I'm here, aren't I? I'd give it all up for your mom to get better. Just like I am doing right now!" I started bawling and left the car for my front door. Jett didn't follow, and once I had the door open, he drove off.

"Lord, I don't know what just happened, but is Jett pushing me away? I understand his pain and grief—but please, soften his heart to understand mine." I spent another hour in prayer and reflection. Had I treated Jett like he was just "part of the master plan"? Was I always open and honest with him about my feelings? Was I open and honest with myself—did I love Jett?

I knew I had some job searching to do, so while I reflected on the matter, it was time to get ready for that. No matter what happened, I needed money for survival, as I was there for the next six months, regardless. And off to a great start, clearly.

As I washed my hair, I thought of all the reasons to love Jett. He was gorgeous. Tall, lean, and naturally athletic. He had a brilliant mind and did very well in school. Jett was

Christian, and we shared the same values. I loved his mother like my own.

Okay, that last one made me choke up. Clearly, I felt very strongly for the relationship I had with his mother. But, what happened if she. . . No, I couldn't think about that yet. Right then, I needed to pray for clarity on my relationship with Jett. Did Jett see something I didn't? And if he thought all this time I didn't love him, why was he with me in the first place?

CHAPTER 3:

PARTLY FLUSTERED, MOSTLY IN DENIAL

Without a job, I wouldn't be able to buy groceries. So, I headed out my front door, drawn to the smell of espresso a few doors down.

Slipping into the door of The Rusted Mug, the smell of fresh espresso and baked delights allured my senses. A fresh stack of newspapers was at the register, and the barista, a beautiful brunette with a purple cardigan and bright lipstick greeted me.

"Ah, fresh blood. Are you new in town, or just here to take in the views?"

I laughed at her unexpected greeting. Looking around sheepishly, I whispered back, "New here." I lifted a hand and sheepishly waved. "Was it that obvious?"

"I've known everyone here since one of us was in diapers, so yeah, you and that gorgeous hair of yours stick out like a sore thumb."

"I'm Hailey." I stuck out my hand, to which she reciprocated.

"Carolina. Welcome to the best coffee in Big Horn. It might be because it's the *only* coffee shop that makes an organic roast, but I don't make the rules." She winked. "And surely, you are here to get some caffeine, so what can I get ya, hun?" Her bright red lipstick revealed perfectly white, straight movie star teeth.

As we chatted a little about her coffee selection, I ordered a drip Arabica black coffee and bought a newspaper, so I could begin looking for the classifieds section. The paper was the thinnest one I'd ever felt; heck, even the campus paper we had at Northwoods had more to report than this.

"Here you go, sweets."

"Thank you, Carolina. This is within walking distance of my rental, so you'll be seeing more of me."

"I have no doubt we all will be." Carolina smiled. Though I wasn't entirely sure what she meant, I reciprocated.

Choosing a small table near the door, I tore open the newspaper. The last page finally contained a small section of job postings, along with a few bulletins for cattle auctions, people looking for farm equipment, and a bright, blue tractor for sale.

The job postings were more of the same from what I saw online: energy industry jobs I had no idea about and meat processing plants. But I couldn't believe my eyes when I saw the last one on the page: *"B6 News/Big Horn Newsroom Searching for Weather Reporter—Apply Within."*

My heart picked up the pace as I scrambled to pull out my phone and look up where the newsroom was located. As I typed it into my phone's browser, I got a notification that I was out of roaming data. "No!" I shouted in a moment of zero situational awareness and felt all the eyes in the shop land on me. A shriek was heard two tables over and another woman near the door dropped her phone in the disruption. Carolina walked over to see if I was okay.

"Sorry, it's just my phone is acting up. Could you tell me where the Big Horn Newsroom is? I need directions." The woman, whose name tag read *Carolina*, snorted in laughter.

"You won't need directions for that, dear. Heck, it's two doors down." I perked up, jumping to my feet, as she pointed to the right. Thanking her, I bundled up my newspaper, gulped the last of my coffee, and left. Once I got outside, I looked to the right and saw a familiar satellite dish on the roof, broadcast antennas, and a large sign that read *Bighorn Newsroom*. How on earth did I not see that before?

I straightened my blazer and ran my fingers through my hair. Though I'd only been there one day, I knew my dress slacks and satiny top might have been overdressing for most jobs, except that one. There was one industry where you always dressed up, no matter if your audience was farmers or finance gurus, and that was television networks. Refreshing my sheer lipstick and popping a breath mint after all that black coffee, I was ready to go in. I reached for the door handle and found out that it was locked. Locked? Were they *closed?*

I checked my watch—it was noon on a Tuesday. Why would they be closed? Out of the corner of my eye, I saw a woman walking to her car from around the building.

"Excuse me, miss? Do you know the hours of the station? I'm here to apply for a job." The woman turned to me, smiling so wide, it was almost frightening, as she obviously looked me up and down.

"Well, aren't you just a peach? It's open, dear. That front door is just closed for the wind. You must not be from around here? You gotta go around to the side door. It won't get caught in one of our gusts and break off, taking you with it."

The air was as calm as could be, but I didn't give her words much thought. "I'm the station secretary, Nancy, and I just know I'll be seeing you again." With a wink, she opened her car door and climbed inside.

"Thank you!" I took off, going around the side of the building, elated to find a nice side door with two potted plants outside of it and a flashing sign that said *OPEN.* Stepping inside, it felt nearly deserted compared to the campus news station. Sure, the college population was greater than that whole town's count, but I was starting to worry no one was there, when I finally heard footsteps.

A mid-thirties man with round, black rimmed glasses and soft black hair emerged. My first thought was that he looked like Keanu Reeves, but immediately, his high, nasal-pitched voice dispelled that thought. "Hello. Can I help you?"

"Hi there. Hailey Sinclair," I reached to shake his hand, which he cautiously accepted, "I'm here to apply for the position of weather reporter." His handshake became a little more eager once I said that, and he released my hand, running his hand through his beautiful hair.

"I thought you were selling Girl Scout cookies or something." I blinked. Was that a joke? An insult? Both?

"Oh?" It wasn't clear to me what about my appearance made him think that, but I let him continue without saying anything else.

"Nice to meet you, Hailey. I'm Nick Taylor, station manager. Tell me about yourself." I smiled, relieved I hadn't just almost pitched my résumé to the vending machine guy.

"I just graduated from Northwood U in Oregon with my degree in Meteorology."

Nick's eyes grew wide with the revelation. "And you're *here?* May I ask why?"

I nodded in reply. "Family member—er—my boyfriend's mom is really sick. I moved here to be closer to her." Short and sweet.

"I get it. Wow, I don't know if we've ever had a real meteorologist on staff before." I felt my eyes bug out of my head. I knew it was rural, but I was excited to be the first, if I got the job, that was. "Of course, we've always had the infamous Donny Gray. He can predict weather in his bad knee, with a 75% accuracy rate. But we've just promoted him to head anchor after Bob finally quit."

"Oh, I'm sorry to hear that."

"About Donny or Bob?" Nick smiled at me. I could see he was the playful type. "No worries. Bob is 93 years old and well, was just so loved here that no one wanted to take his job away. Truthfully, he wanted to retire since he was in his early 70's. He tried to call in sick every single morning, but the station manager, Carla, had a pretty big crush on him, so she begged him to come in. They eventually got married, and their entire lives were here, so he figured he may as well take home a paycheck, too. But a week ago, he finally got the nerve to quit for good, after Carla decided to retire."

"Makes sense. Sounds like there's a lot of longevity with staff here. It must be a nice place to work?" My mind started to wander as I looked around. While Nick went on about the workplace culture, saying the staff "really is a family," I started to wonder if the station was depressing or exciting. Though this wasn't the scale I was expecting, or used to, as even my college station was larger, I decided it wouldn't be so bad to spend a few months here. If anything, I could bring a new standard of weather reporting to the community.

"It's the best place to work in Big Horn, I can promise you that."

So why are they hiring at all, I wondered?"

"Let's just say, most of our kids move out and never return. Chasing those big city dreams."

I realized I must have asked the question aloud and winced at his reply. Triggered, I was. I couldn't imagine coming there *for real* after college. No, this was just for then. Not forever.

I took a breath, letting go of pride and protocol. "I'd like the job—if you'll have me." I put my hand out to Nick for his shake. Normally, I wouldn't be so forward and let the job offers come to me. But, with the enormity of what I had riding on this, paired with very little in my bank account, I decided food and running water were a priority that I needed to fight for. Nick looked at my hand as if he was analyzing the mysteries of the universe, but he did return the handshake.

We agreed that I would start the next morning, and he would give me the lay of the land, along with our schedules for news then. It wasn't much, but it was a start that I felt very, very thankful for.

Returning back to the rental, I looked around in the daylight. The paint on the rental's trim was peeling, and a lone garden gnome sat in the empty flower beds. On closer inspection, he was missing an arm. His eyes bore into me like he'd seen too much. I shuddered, before going back inside to see everything else in the daylight since I had been caffeinated.

Studying my surroundings, there was something so depressing about it, but the more I thought about it, the more I realized it felt empty and deflated because it was. Since I had gotten a job and a lease that would charge me hand over fist to break early, I knew my time there would at least last six months, so why wouldn't I make the most of it?

An extra set of taupe sheets worked perfectly to cover up the deflated couch, even holding in some of its stuffing so it looked a little more shapely. My favorite peach fuzzy blanket and throw pillows, that looked like succulents, modernized it overall. I hung a canvas above it; one that I created at a one-off painting class I took on campus, as part of a fundraiser one of the committees was putting on. It was an abstract landscape that looked like all four seasons at once.

The small, round dining room table adjacent to the living room became home to a few of my assorted candle holders. Below them, I laid a round, lace doily that used to sit on my nightstand when I was a child. A set of curtains I made in a weekend sewing class at the recreation center near campus fit perfectly above the small kitchen window.

There was a small, built-in bookshelf in the tiny bedroom. On the shelves, I placed my childhood scrapbook, an assortment of meteorology books from school that I paid a handsome sum for that I wanted to keep, and finally, my Bible. The scraggly potted plants I'd managed to somewhat keep alive over the years fit nicely on the shelves, too, and on the bottom of the box, I found a worn copy of Dana Summers autobiography, *"Making Sunshine."* I remembered finding it in my mother's possessions after I lost her to cancer, and it somewhat cemented my interest in meteorology, becoming a weather forecaster, and in all things Dana, of course.

Opening boxes that I'd been packing over the last few weeks was strange. Funny, though those things had been in my life for as long as I could remember, as I pulled each of them out, it was like I was seeing them for the first time.

A framed portrait of my mother went on the small mantel above the fireplace. While I was at it, I noticed a few logs inside the brick chamber, so I crumpled up some of the newspaper I had used for packing and lit it. It was cozy and warm. I stood by the flames, staring deeply into the picture of my mother that had been taken at one of those mall photoshoot places where they doll you up into a movie star. Tears welled in my eyes as I remembered her.

"If I could have done things differently, I would've been a weather girl. Just like Dana Summers." My mother's voice carried into the hallway, from where she was speaking on the

telephone next to her bedside. "Wouldn't that have been something?" I knew from the candid conversation that she'd been speaking with one of her gal pals from high school. Those days, in between spending time with me and my father and in the Bible, she was doing a lot of reminiscing. "But God had other plans for me." I peeked into her room, seeing her pick up a portrait of me that was on her nightstand. She was lying in bed but wearing her signature bright pink blush, taupe eyeshadow and lots of mascara. Tears rolled down her cheeks as she lay the portrait beside her. "Well, I better get to it." She paused. "Don't forget me, Susan." Her expression was morose. "You better promise!" She smiled, but it didn't reach her eyes. "I love you, too. Buh-bye."

The small cat clock I'd hung on the wall just an hour before starting meowing. It was four in the afternoon, and I'd told Cindy I'd be by around then for our movie night. I quickly washed my face and refreshed my soft makeup, pulled my wild mane of curls into a top knot, and slipped on white tennis shoes over my thick socks. Turning the small brass doorknob to leave, a giant blast of wind yeeted the door all the way open. While not much went through my mind in the process, I instinctively held onto the doorknob like it was the last lifeboat on the Titanic, and the deflated couch caught me as the door tossed me aside. The door whipped back and forth a few times as I started to uncontrollably laugh. "If only I had a bad knee to sense that was coming," I hollered out the door, no one around to hear me. My closest neighbors' homes had no sign of life, except for a rusty bicycle in the yard.

When the air calmed enough that I could close the door and latch it, jiggling it a few times to ensure it wouldn't blow open like it paid my rent, I headed for Jett's house, hoping to remember the path we took yesterday. When I got out on the main road, however, I quickly noticed there was only *one* road that went in either direction, so sure enough, I found the place easily.

I knew things weren't going well that day when I saw the expression on Jett's face as he opened the door. His eyes were red, and it looked like it had been days since he'd last shaved.

"Hi." I leaned in to give him a deep hug, which he gently reciprocated. "Not good?" I whispered, but he didn't respond.

"Is that Hailey?" A cheerful voice called from the kitchen. I was taken aback by Cindy's glowing appearance and looked back at Jett.

"I'm here for a movie night." Cindy looked joyful to see me, though Jett still had a look of surprise on his face. In my hand was a copy of *Dirty Dancing* that I'd brought from home.

"That's wonderful, dear. Why don't you two clear and set the table while we finish making dinner? Bruce is just finishing up the spaghetti. I'm garnishing the garlic bread." My stomach growled at the thought, while I realized I was starving. I nodded, pleased to be able to have a conversation with Jett. He disappeared into the kitchen with the dishes, returning to the dining room with clean cutlery, plates and napkins.

"How are you doing?" I asked him as he set the plates down, putting my arm around his neck and kissing his cheek. His body stiffened, and I pulled away.

"I'm alright." Shrugging off my question, he looked exhausted.

As we sat down for dinner, breathing in the aroma of spaghetti with extra parmesan, I relished in the nurturing, loving environment that Jett's parents' house was. Though things weren't well, that night, it felt like more than enough to just be together.

"I got a job today," I casually mentioned. Cindy's eyes looked electric.

"Really! Already? Did you hear that, Bruce? Tell me everything, Hailey!"

"Yep. Down at the Big Horn Newsroom. Kind of random how they were looking for a weather reporter right when I got here, actually." I took a moment of reflection on just how God was moving mountains for me. Jett was about to take a bite of a meatball when I dropped the news, and his jaw was ajar as I spoke.

"Isn't that incredible? Tell me more about that, Hailey." Cindy was my biggest cheerleader at that table, and Jett's silence was starting to irk me.

"The previous reporter, um. . .Donny? He got promoted to anchor, so that leaves it to me to predict the weather in Big Horn, Wyoming!" The table broke out into giggles and even Jett got in on the laughter. When it didn't die down, I asked what was so funny.

"Oh, Donny was quite possibly the worst weather reporter in the world!" The table was cackling so hard, Bruce could barely stammer out his words. "He used to get his reports from Montana, who had a meteorologist that would send him reports, right? Well, they had a falling out, and for the last few years, Bruce has been reporting based on the hunch he gets from his arthritic joints." I too, started to laugh when I heard that.

After dinner, Cindy and Bruce retired to the back porch around their fire pit. When Jett tried to join them, she shooed him away. "Honey, I love you here, but your father and I haven't had a single moment to ourselves." She winked at me when she spoke, the light shining so bright from her, it was both beautiful and crushing at the same time because of how much she meant to everyone. "Why don't you and Hailey go for a walk? Or show her that coin collection you've been working on since you were seven years old. For all the Saturdays we spent helping you find those things, I'd like to see you use them to impress a girl at least once."

Jett laughed, but there was such a sadness in him that I felt guilty for taking him away from them.

"You know what? I have a big day tomorrow, being my first day at the station. I'll leave you guys to it. Thank you for having me over for dinner." I quickly hugged them before they had a chance to object, but deep down, I knew Jett wouldn't, and I didn't know why, but a part of me didn't want to, either.

Tears rolled down my cheeks as I got into my car. I could feel things happening in our relationship, all of which made me feel very out of control. A feeling I was not able to cope with well. On the drive home, I passed a worn-out sign with half of the letters out of order. From what I could read, it said "World's Best Cinnamon Rolls." I pulled a U-turn so fast, half of my hair flopped over my eyes, causing me to over-correct by braking. Fast. The maneuver resulted in a loud screech of burning tires, all the heads in the well-lit cafe turning on me, and suddenly, I was looking very *desperate* for a cinnamon roll. I considered giving them a few minutes to forget what had just happened, but when they all continued eating their very delicious-looking concoctions with eyes on me, I just went for it.

If the attention wasn't already on me, the loud bell that chimed when I walked in made sure everyone got another look. "Table for one, please." The stunning waitress, name-tag reading *Georgianna,* took one look at my tear-stained cheeks and nodded. Her bright red locks were twisted up into a banana clip. She looked about my age, with a soft peach glow to her skin. Her bright green eyes were kind as she took me to a corner booth. The diner was beautifully retro, and a real reprieve for my tired eyes. This was that far the nicest place I'd visited in an otherwise deserted town. The seats were upholstered in turquoise sparkle vinyl, the kind of material that sticks to your skin on hot days.

"Here you go. Can I help you with anything?" I was surprised at her question, that felt both personable and inquisitive, rather than just taking an order, but I didn't want to spill my deepest feelings to a stranger just yet.

"I'd like one of those 'Worlds' Best Cinnamon Rolls,' please." She smiled, pleased to have the order. She spun on her heels, her figure petite. I watched her go to the glass case behind the counter and look at each roll, as if choosing the right one that would have an impact on my evening. She placed a fat, round roll with copious amounts of glaze on a bright floral plate and turned her back to me to do something else. From there, she looked like a beautiful fairy.

After she set down the larger-than-life cinnamon roll that I could have probably made into three meals, a large cup of hot cocoa was set before me, as she topped it right there with a bottle of whip cream that was in her apron pocket. "This one's on the house," she said as she took the menu off of my table and spun around, instantaneously laughing glamorously at a handsome man who was waving his hand to get her attention. He stood, kissing her on the cheek, before taking her hands and pretending to slow dance with her. I couldn't help but smile as I looked at those two, who seemed madly in love.

Watching them brought a feeling of dread as I thought of my own relationship.

The devil is in the comparison, I told myself. But Jett and I had never been like that. Not only had we never spontaneously danced, but we'd never *laughed* like that. After cutting into my cinnamon roll, I tore out the center, which was bigger than I thought, but since no one was looking, and I'd been watching my figure since I was twelve, I went for it. As soon as it touched my taste buds, I felt like I'd died and gone to heaven. I let out an "mmm" noise, as the comfort from the sugary delight was just what I needed. A man sitting at the diner's bar stools across from me spun around and looked at me.

"You've got something there." He motioned to my cheek, while I was caught off guard by his handsomely rugged look. I didn't notice him from behind, not that I was looking, but I instantly wished my mouth wasn't as full as it was. Chipmunks could learn from how much I had piled in right then. I tried to chew some more down before I acknowledges the handsome gentleman speaking to me, and eventually, I wiped my cheek with the bright turquoise napkins. "No, not that side. The other cheek." I was still chewing and was starting to feel a little irked that the guy was *bothering* me. I gave a polite wave, as if to say, "thanks, but no thanks," but that didn't do the trick. I finally finished chewing that monstrous bite, took the napkin, and wiped my entire face with it.

"Did I get it?" I almost yelled back, unintentionally. I startled myself with how impatient I sounded, and it filled me with instant regret. I would never raise my voice at Jett, and him coming to mind right then reminded me I was sitting in a diner alone in his hometown. Those folks may not have known me, but they likely knew him and his family, and then I remembered they were all about to learn who I was if they paid attention to the news. But the guy wasn't deterred in the slightest.

"Let me get a closer look." I watched him as he slid off the stool and into the other side of the booth. I was a little uncertain with his motives and uncomfortable with how that may have appeared to others, but the chances of Jett suddenly wanting to see me and come to look for me there were slim to zero. "Alright, you got it. But there's still some eye stuff, maybe?"

"Eye stuff?" I wiped my finger along my eyelid, instantly filled with regret. I forgot I put on mascara and eyeliner earlier that day for my job search, and so, mixed with my tears, the napkin started the freefall. "Isn't that just perfect." I grumpily set down the napkin, taking another huge, unforgiving bite of my cinnamon roll, ignoring the handsome stranger and the scale of which he was.

"I appreciate a woman who can eat." I expected the man to be put off, but instead, his light brown eyes that reminded me of the interior of a luxury sports car were all over me, and I didn't want to enjoy it as much as I did.

"I have a boyfriend." His smile got even wider as I continued to gorge on my cinnamon roll, not even attempting to be lady-like in any manner. Chugging the hot chocolate next, I peeked over the rim of the mug and noticed his chestnut hair looked a little more red in the light. His scruffy beard, I estimated a good two days' worth, was a dead giveaway he was single. I personally would not want to kiss a man with a beard. But why was I thinking about kissing that man? I slammed the mug down, empty, fully aware I had whipped cream on my upper lip and nose and zero idea of why I was behaving that way. This was so, completely, unequivocally unlike me. But there was something about that man that brought out an unfamiliar feeling in me. Just looking at him, I felt irritated. Crazy. And like the most beautiful woman in the world.

"I have a secret for you." His eyes searched mine for answers, when he was the one sharing the riddle. Never before had I had someone look so deeply into my soul.

"I can't keep a secret to save my life," I quipped back. It was true, but mostly because I'd never been asked to keep one. He had a smooth laugh that revealed he had a gold tooth on one of his front molars. It worked for him—made him feel even more cowboy or something.

"I was hoping you'd say that—because this secret ain't for keepin'." Color me intrigued.

"Okay, I'll bite." I set down my fork for the first time since the cinnamon roll was placed before me and gave him my undivided attention. I felt extremely uneasy—like how I imagined Adam and Eve felt in the garden when they realized they were naked. This guy could see right through me, in parts of me I didn't even know were there, and I didn't like it. Not one bit.

"I know something that's going to happen in the future." If I had milk to shoot out my nose, it would have. Suddenly, I was wondering what exactly I was doing there, and I waved to the waitress, so I could get the check, but her back was to me.

"There's no such thing as psychics. No one knows the future except God." I shut him down royally, hard and fast, but he didn't quit.

"I agree with you there. This isn't so much a psychic thing as it is an extreme faith that what God has planned will come to pass."

"So, a man of faith?" It made him even more annoyingly attractive knowing he was a Christian. "Okay, what is it that you see right now?" I tilted my head at him, taking another bite of the gooey cinnamon roll that I couldn't get enough of.

"I can't tell you that just yet." He dropped that statement like an anvil, got up, and walked away. I noticed he was in wrangler jeans, a plaid long-sleeve button up, and a Carhartt vest. He retrieved a cowboy hat from a hat stand by the door. As I sat and watched him interact for a few moments with Georgianna, I noticed how good the hat looked on him, and then he left the dine—but first, gave me a wink. I felt angry at his lack of boundaries. Or was it something else?

I finished chewing my bite, when I realized how ridiculous it was that I was just sitting there with my mouth full, then Georgianna promptly came over. "How was everything?" She was grinning, revealing a bright white, gap tooth smile. "It sounds like you made an impression on someone tonight."

"Geez. Who is that guy, anyway? I told him I have a boyfriend, but he just wouldn't leave me alone. Telling me he can see the future? Please! I'm sure he uses that line on every woman he sees." Georgianna's jaw dropped.

"What did that fella say he saw?" I noticed a little drawl to her words as she spoke.

"After all that, he wouldn't even tell me. The nerve of him!" Georgianna's eyes widened, along with her smile.

"Girl, you made an impression all right." She let out a low whistle. "Anyway, he took care of your cinnamon roll and wanted to make sure I sent you home with another. Said you got a real appetite on you." She placed a white paper bag on my table. "Can I get you anything else?"

"Of course he did. Something about that guy just irks me." I was secretly flattered he covered my roll and got me another. But something about him was s. . . Disruptive to my evening.

"If that ain't love. . .Girl, you rolled up in this diner tonight like a hurricane in a corn field. Plus, you're crazy gorgeous. If half the men in here weren't old enough to be your paw and the other half weren't taken, including that hunk right there to yours truly," she pointed at the man I saw her dancing with earlier, and I smiled, "there would have been more suitors for you to choose from. It was bound to happen that someone would take notice."

"It *was* kind of an embarrassing entrance." I laughed, and she let out the giggle she'd been holding back the whole conversation. "Are you married?" I pointed to the ring on her finger.

"Sure am, for two months now. He moved me halfway across the country here to be with him; it's the least he could do to build me this diner, don't you think? He's just got to get his rear in gear and fix my sign. The dang storm last week nearly took the whole thing out. Half my letters ain't workin,' but that's okay because all people gotta know is 'World's Best Cinnamon Rolls,' and that part's workin' peachy keen."

I was overjoyed to hear that Georgianna owned the diner. I looked at the sign outside closer and could see the place was called "Georgianna's." With her red hair and the sparkling turquoise surroundings, she reminded me of a mermaid.

"I used to work at a place like this in Louisiana; of course, it wasn't this nice. It ain't anything like this—it was a real dive, actually. But the secret is in the cinnamon roll. It's my recipe, and they always begged me for it, but I wouldn't give it. It stays with me. This place, yeah, this is just what Wyoming needed. And heck, I think it's the only place open after six in the evening. These folk really know how to turn in early."

Georgianna had a great conversation after an irritating evening. She refilled my hot chocolate, and despite having consumed enough sugar for the next month, the comfort the warm cup brought me was immeasurable.

It was clear something was going on with Jett, and I had come to have an annoying guy paying attention to me. But he didn't cross any lines by asking for my phone number, I supposed. That was something I noticed. He just left, with no expectation of calling me, which was good because if he did ask, I would have turned him down. What part of "boyfriend" does that guy not understand? The more I thought about it, the more I wondered what it was about that guy that made me feel that way.

I finished up my hot chocolate and watched the place empty out. Only a few people remained, including Georgianna's husband, who was now taking out the garbage. As the last tables were paying, I took the cue and left a cash tip on the table and left. The next morning was my first day at my new job, and I had better get some sleep.

CHAPTER 4:

A LITTLE CHAOS, A LITTLE CHARM

The morning after my cinnamon roll feast, I felt the sugar hangover draining my energy. Funny how that has always worked. It took more determination to drag myself into my first day than normal.

"Move a little more to the right, Hailey." Nick guided me around the green screen. "Right there. Let's actually mark that spot on the floor. Tommy? Where's that roll of tape you had?"

As everyone showed me the ropes of the station, I prayed for my own disappointment. I didn't want to feel that way. Despite always believing there was something greater out in the world for me, a grand stage to do the weather, if you will—I didn't want that steppingstone to bring me down. My biggest fear was being stuck in a town like that forever. But then again, judging by how things were going with Jett, there was a slim chance our relationship was going to make it anyway. That realization gutted me, but stoicism was my greatest trait—up until the prior night, that was. I still felt puffy from eating that giant cinnamon roll—and the other one for breakfast, but I'd do it again. And was heavily considering doing so that evening, in fact, after I visited Cindy.

"Tommy, put the tape right where Hailey is standing, would you? A big 'X', so she can't miss it." Nick's high-pitched voice was nails on a chalkboard the day before, but that day, it was lessened. Or maybe, I was used to it.

"Okay, Hailey. We're all set for tonight's forecast. Why don't you come with me, and I'll show you our computer room, where you can do research and all that forecasting stuff."

I was elated to hear there was a room for me to do that there, as I didn't have wi-fi at my rental, and I sure as heck couldn't figure things out on my phone. I needed computer programs to do that. In fact, I had everything I needed written down and was prepared to give it to Nick.

When we reached the room, it was better than I'd hoped. A double monitor setup and a nice large desk with an ergonomic chair. There was even a large window facing a mountain, which was probably how Donny Gray's infamous forecasts were decided.

"Thank you, Nick. This will do." I pulled out my list and crossed off the things I saw that were already provided. "I'm just going to need a few software's installed before I can get to work. Some of them are free, but some cost. Given that I'm not an independent weather contractor, can I expect the station to foot the bill?" Nick ran his fingers through his hair, clearly reconsidering what it meant to have a "real meteorologist" on staff.

"Umm, I mean, if you need them, right? We definitely want you to have what you need. What might these software's cost?"

I'd never actually seen hair stand up on the back of someone's neck before. But since Nick had a clean-shaven neck, appearing that he got a haircut the day before after we met- I could only imagine what it would have looked like if he hadn't gotten all the baby hairs shaved off. They would have been waving at me.

After some back and forth, we discovered there were a few free versions of software, and the only one I absolutely couldn't budge on was a little under a thousand dollars. Sure, he didn't want to pay for it, but I assured him a real news agency would have this software. That did the trick.

Nick wanted more than anything to appear like a reputable station. And truthfully, it wasn't missing much. The equipment wasn't downright shoddy, at least not what I'd discovered so far. I had doubts about the cameraman after our test shoot, considering he cut the top of my head out of the frame, but apparently he was just filling in for the regular camera man, Colt, who was out on leave. Something about moving cows. The cows—not like the picturesque white cows with black spots but rather big, black angus cows—they were moving to a different pasture for the summer. Apparently, the cameraman was also a rancher? I didn't get the gist of it, but at that point, I didn't need to. I just needed to focus on things happening right now. We only had two forecasts a day, the morning one could be prerecorded, but our evening news was live. As he explained it to me, I'd be doing more outdoor assignments than I expected.

"Despite our small population, we actually have quite a bit of things going on that I think you'll find interesting. For instance, we had a windstorm rip the roof off of the old Rimrock Ranger Station last month. With Donny's bad knee, he couldn't make the trip out there. I'd love it if you were able to report on that."

"Let me get this straight—the wind. . .*Ripped the roof. . .off. . .of a building?*" Just repeating the words made me feel dizzy. I looked outside again and things were as calm as a daylily. What did that place have in store for me?

"Yeah, it sure did. I mean, the roof had it coming. It wasn't properly reinforced with steel. Out here, a roof needs to be engineered for wind and snowpack. It's just a lethal combo when we get a windstorm in the winter. But don't worry, we're in the nice season now. We still have a few months to worry about winter."

"A few months? It's only June!" I felt my voice become shrill, and Nick nodded.

"A weather dork like you is going to love this: We've had snow on the ground on the Fourth of July before. That's pretty dang early, or pretty dang late, however the year goes. It isn't abnormal to get our first blizzard around Labor Day. This isn't the tropics, that's for sure. You'll have plenty to report on." With a laugh, he spun on his heels and left me to work.

Nick shut the door to my computer room as I started pounding away on the keys to bring up the weather models and visualizing software. Looking over to the window, the air was still calm as ever, and I was starting to wonder if the infamous wind there was just a giant ruse they were playing on me. Turned out, the calm was just a Wyoming bluff.

After I prepared the weather forecast, I couldn't help but feel it was very mundane. I was okay with that; however, as that would be the first forecast on live television that would go out to people who weren't at my university, I'd have rather it be boring than have something go awry. Saying a joke that didn't land. Accidentally getting myself cancelled by mispronouncing a word. There were just too many variables. Yes, boring and mundane was the way. I chose a demure outfit, a navy blazer over a white top and khaki slacks. I was wearing my signature sky high heels, as I had to be somewhat dressed up. It was still television, no matter where I was. And at my next job interview, I would be sharing clips from this to audition. Realizing that made this whole experience a little more fun for me, so I leaned into that. I would treat the experience as one long audition tape for where I really needed to be: in the big city, somewhere, anywhere. Away from there.

We had just a few more minutes until show time, so I went into the only room that had bright lighting for a makeup artist and touched up my lipstick and mascara. The makeup artist was the one thing I wasn't sad about, considering I preferred to do my own, but I did wish there had been someone there to help me wrangle my hair. I opted to wear it down, applying heavy amounts of curl cream to eliminate frizz. It was still huge, but I tossed it to one side, and I was happy with it.

"It's showtime, Hailey. Just like we discussed, Donny will start the evening, share one story, and I will give you a five second countdown on my hands. When I get to one, consider the camera rolling. We fixed the issue with our fill-in camera man, so don't worry; your whole head will be in the picture." Nick started laughing again, which made me chuckle in reply, letting off a little steam. It felt good to laugh for a minute, and the night started on a sweet note.

"Good evening and welcome to the five-o-clock news for Big Horn, Wyoming." A soft, tasteful ballad played, and the cameraman changed angles, Donny shifting his upper body to meet it. All in all, it was more professional than I expected, and suddenly I felt a little nervous. "Tonight's top story involves a harrowing tale of a rancher getting tossed from his cow. According to Thad Newman—rancher, husband, and father— his cow had tolerated being saddled many times, until it didn't. We are going to show a clip of the incident, but viewer discretion is advised: This may be upsetting."

As the clip rolled, I got a good look at Donny, who was straightening his papers on the news desk. We hadn't formally met until about ten minutes before, and the introduction was on the fly. His tan suit complimented his dark blonde hair and tan skin, and his eyes were a pale green. Nick told me he spent his days playing pickleball and didn't show up to set until the very last minute, but I wouldn't have known that by how prepared he seemed. All in all, he gave a great show, which made me increasingly nervous to make my debut. But my time to worry was up, because Nick was giving me the countdown.

"Now, let's go to the weather with meteorologist Hailey Sinclair." Nick held up one finger, and then none. But the words were slow to come out. I looked at the screen blankly until my brain caught up with me.

"Thank you, Donny." I spoke slowly and robotically. "My name is Hailey Sinclair, and I just moved here." Ugh. That was not in my script. "And tonight, we are forecasting some very tumultuous weather this week. It looks like gusts up to forty miles per hour. Batten down the hatches, but it will be a bright, beautiful day reaching a high of fifty-nine, no clouds in sight. Because with those wind gusts, they all blow away. Some showers later in the week, however—not to worry—we'll have plenty of outside time this weekend as it will reach into the seventies. There looks to be a coming inversion for next Monday, however, with lows back in the twenties." As I recited the weather I had researched earlier, suddenly, something clicked in my mind. "For June? I don't know how you guys put up with this." Wait, did I say that out loud? Oh no! "But of course, it's worth it, because it's so—Wyoming is just so—" *Think, think, think, Hailey! What word describes this place?* "Cowboy." My face turned fifty shades of red. I really could have gone for some of that mortuary makeup right about then as I scrambled to end my segment. "And back to you, Donny." I shifted my body towards him, though he was sitting off-screen, as I gave an unplanned *thumbs up* to the cameraman. *Wait—I was supposed to say commercial break!* I'd blown the whole thing just like that. As the cameraman changed back to Donny, he covered my butt.

"We'll be back in just a few minutes." The *ON-AIR* light flashed off, and I breathed for a moment, expecting Nick to come hand me a pink slip.

The silence in the studio could've filled a canyon. *Cowboy? What even was that? I might as well have said "yeehaw" and galloped off the set.*

"Believe it or not, I've seen worse." Nick came and patted me on the shoulder, while one of the stage hands, Maria, backed him up.

"I actually liked how real you were, Hailey. I don't know how I put up with this weather to be honest. I have no reason to live here at all. My dogs don't even like it. It's just the job, and I could probably find another—," she stopped short as Nick piped up.

"Now, now, let's not make a rash decision here. You're my favorite here, Maria, and I can't live without those enchilada's you bring on Fridays. I'm sure your husband enjoys his friends and family here, right? And doesn't his mother live with you here to stay close to his and her friends?"

"Like I said, I have no reason to be here at all. Zero. Zilch. *Get me away from that woman.*"

"Your mother in law?" Nick asked innocently, but Maria mouthed back to me something about how she couldn't stand the woman. I giggled at the thought.

"Thank you both for the encouragement. I'd like to think I was a little more prepared, but when push came to shove, I was a disaster." Truthfully, I didn't care. Though I had decided earlier to treat this job like an interview for the big city stations, it couldn't be more obvious how disconnected I felt.

"Did you give that ranger station roof story any thought, Hailey? Normally we also have a few special interest pieces like that a week."

"Yes, it will be no problem. I just need to coordinate with the cameraman. In fact, I'll get his phone number at the end of the show so we can make a plan for tomorrow."

"That's excellent, Hailey. But don't bother with Ben, our fill in. Here, let me write down Colt's phone number for you. He's our full-time guy, and much more capable." He leaned in a little closer to whisper. "I'm not sure that our Benny boy here can see colors. I don't discriminate, of course, but it certainly helps to not be colorblind in the television world."

"Great," I said. Taking the paper from his hands, I folded it up and put it in my pocket. "I'll give him a call. Unless he's busy wrangling animals?" Nick had explained about the cows earlier, and didn't mention how long he'd be on leave.

"He is supposed to be back on Monday, so there's no rush. It's a few day cattle drive, but he's still in cell phone service, and he's got his truck with him, so he's home every night."

I gave Nick a nod before he went back to give Donny the countdown. The commercial break dragged on, but Nick explained earlier how they were chock full of farm store and tractor ads. There was a local production company that shot the commercials, and it was also led by Colt. He sure was a jack of all trades. Donny prepared to start again.

"Welcome back to the five-o-clock news. Our next story is a bit of an unbelievable tale, but we assure you it's entirely true." He paused to give a professional laugh. "For the case of Tally Abrams, her dog, Roofus, a three-year-old Weimaraner, has formed an unlikely bond with a local goose at the duck pond. Going so far as the goose landing in her backyard." As Donny went on, I moved off my stand to watch the rest of the program to get a better grip on cues and Donny's style.

After the show, I asked for a few tapes on Donny's forecasts to get an idea of what they were like. Nick had some rolling footage to show me then and there, but nothing I could take home.

"If you want, come this weekend, say tomorrow; I'd be happy to show you Donny and Bob's show. But tonight, I gotta get out of here." He paused, and I had a feeling he wanted me to ask why, but when I didn't, because it's none of my business, he offered anyway. "I have a hot date." Nick straightened his checkered tie and slicked back the sides of his hair.

"Good for you." I smiled, unsure what to do at that moment with my new boss. Replay that cringe thumbs-up? Offer a high five? Tell him his outfit totally clashed, and he had better go home and change, lest she might think he was dressed by a five year old? Instead, I did nothing, and he continued to talk. "She's finally agreed to go out with me after a year of my asking her out. There's a lot riding on this date; I need it to be perfect."

"Where are you taking her?"

"To the Italian joint on the corner, then we're going to the roller rink. Or, the other way around. I haven't quite decided." A flashback from my seventh birthday at a roller rink crept up in my memory.

"Take her skating first. You do not want to be full while roller skating. And I am free this weekend; I'll come by tomorrow afternoon if that's good for you." I gave him a pat on the shoulder and told him good night and good luck. It was time to visit Jett's house.

As I left the station, a few wind gusts picked up, and I started to wonder what I was in for. Driving across a small bridge in a canyon, a cross wind came, and I felt the car swerve into the median. "Whew! Giddy up!" I hollered out, feeling shaken. It scared me, and I tightened my grip on the steering wheel and said a prayer to God for protection. My reliable Ford Explorer had been hardy enough to handle hail, snow, and torrential downpours, but I had never driven in high winds like those that sounded to be common there.

Arriving at Jett's, all of the lights were on inside. The sun wouldn't set for another hour at least. It looked like dinner had just ended, and I saw his family inside playing a game of Monopoly. Gazing at Cindy, she looked joyful as she held up some colorful money while Bruce waved her off. Jett was laughing, but even from the curb, I could feel his sadness. I questioned if I should interrupt, suddenly feeling like an outsider to this family, so I contemplated my place.

Jett and I weren't married, but we had been dating for three years. His mother and I had become very close, arguably much more than Jett and I had ever been. Jett assumed we would be broken up by him not leaving for Chicago with me, and my being there took him by surprise. Did he want me there at all? Did Cindy need me there? Did any of them? I turned around, walking back to my car parked on the street with the realization that they did not.

I was starting the engine when Bruce popped his head out the front door. I paused, allowing him to walk to my passenger side door instead of taking off. He tapped on the window, and I unlocked it, watching his tall, oversized frame climb into my car.

"Good evening, Hailey. We saw you on the news tonight, and we couldn't be more proud of you." He spoke surely, and his small, rimmed eyeglasses made his squinty eyes appear larger.

"Thank you, Bruce."

"I'm guessing you're feeling a little confused by everything, or you wouldn't be sitting on my curb right now."

"You guessed right." I kept my gaze straight ahead, looking out at the valley their plot was a part of.

"In the same way that you've always known what you wanted, with the strength and determination of a warrior to get there, Jett has been the opposite. Even as a kid, he would wrestle with his mind for an hour over what flavor of ice cream to get." I turned to Bruce, leaning my head on the wheel like a pillow. He was looking at the house. "I think his love for his mom is the only thing he's sure about right now. But I know he loves you, Hailey. So don't take that wrong. Personally, I think he's going to come to his senses sooner than later once he gets bored of hanging around mom and dad. This is just Jett showing his grief. He's pushing you away. I see it plain as day. But you have the option to stay beside him or drive away right now. This is your life, too." Bruce gave my shoulder a squeeze and climbed back out of the car. He hesitated at the sidewalk to see if I would follow, and after a moment of silence, my body robotically climbed out of the car, and I went with him inside.

Cindy welcomed me with open arms, as usual, and Jett even walked up and gave me a hug, which nearly surprised me after the last few days of feeling like it was forced. A small peck on the forehead made me feel like desert rain after a drought. My soul felt brighter, I was at peace, and then I held his hand on the couch while we watched the rerun of the news Cindy had recorded. We all laughed together as I went on my little weather rant, and Bruce and Cindy had a bunch of questions for the production side of things. My heart was full. I almost hated to ruin it by asking Jett if we could talk after, but he surprisingly obliged.

"How are you doing?" I asked him as we sat on his parents' rickety front porch. The white paint was peeling in parts, and it took all the willpower I had not to peel back a layer with my fingertips, as the paint was probably lead.

"I'm okay." I waited for him to say something else. He had so many options—he could ask me how I was, for one. How my day was, how the move had been on me. But instead, we sat in silence. After several minutes of that, I looked up to the sky. The sun had set, and Jett's parents' porchlight was the only light for miles in the valley. A shooting star flashed across the sky.

"Wow! Look at that!" I pointed up, and he excitedly looked up with me, and we started to see star after star shooting around the sky. I was reminded of the magnificence of God's creation, and how in all of that beauty, He created me and cared for me every step of the way, which brought tears to my eyes. Jett looked at me and wiped my gentle tears away while putting his arm around me while we looked.

"I don't know what to do, Hailey." I turned to Jett, and watched his lips move. Both of my arms instinctively wrapped around his waist. I longed for the comfort of his hug, but he didn't hold me any differently, only keeping his arm around me.

"What does that mean for us, Jett?" My voice sounded so. . .desperate. But, I felt desperate, too. I uprooted my life to move out there, only to feel unwanted by the man I wanted to marry. And I still did.

"Can we just slow things down, Hailey? I don't even know what to do here. I still have feelings for you, but I don't think we're on the same page, and I need to be here for my mom." My heart was gutted by his words, but I understood his feelings. When my own mother was dying, my father struggled to do any role other than mourn, and I, too, was having a hard time thinking of myself when knowing Cindy's situation.

"I understand that, Jett, I do. But can you clarify what you mean by not feeling we are on the same page?" Jett sighed, clearly wrestling with how blunt he wanted to be on a topic I was guessing he'd given quite a lot of thought to.

"Hailey, you don't love me; you love the *idea* of me. I was fine with that at first. Heck, you're the total package and the most beautiful woman I've ever seen. But it became clear to me as time went on, and we don't have that deep connection that I need. I want you to want *me,* Hailey. For who I am, not what I'm going to be. Because in a moment, it can all come crumbling apart. I mean, look at me now. I'm twenty-two years old and already put all my plans on hold. I never thought this would happen to my family, but it's given me a lot of time to think about what I need in my life and a partner. I want all or nothing, Hailey. And I wouldn't blame you either way." I pondered his words, grasping each one as they came. While there was plenty of truth to it, I wasn't ready to admit anything to myself. Instead, I was hardheaded in denial.

"I'm here, aren't I? Of course I love you, Jett. I want to get married and be with you forever." Jett smiled, putting his arm around me, and I was filled with relief that my words did the trick.

"I know that's what you think right now, Hailey. But I want you to really consider our relationship and what it is. I think it would be best if we take a break for now and spend some time in our own lives without relying on each other to make ourselves feel better." It was the harshest words he'd ever spoken to me.

"Is this it? Can I still come see Cindy, or do you want me to stay away?" I couldn't bear the thought of not seeing her every day. Jett closed his eyes and shook his head.

"That's another thing. So much of this," he swayed his finger between us, "is based on my mom. That was another thing I loved. But it almost felt too instantaneous. Not that I'm saying it doesn't feel real—you two really act like friends in a past life, not that I believe in that stuff. But if it wasn't for her, would you have stayed with me? I can't answer that." I pulled my head back, suddenly sitting up straight on the porch.

"I'm sorry, Jett." There was no point in denying I was bonded with his mother, but I never intended for him to feel the way he did. "I am with you—er, I was with you, because I love you. And I still do. I think you're the greatest thing since avocado toast." Jett smirked, putting his hands on his knees and looking forward.

"Thank you, Hailey. You are welcome to be here as often as you want. I'm sorry I said that." I stiffly rose to my feet as a huge gust of wind came down the valley, knocking me forward. Jett, who had risen to his feet the moment before, tried to catch me, but he didn't turn fast enough. I landed on the other side of the railing but not before smacking my forehead on a 2x4 railing.

"Are you okay? You're bleeding, Hailey."

As he helped me to my feet, it was all I could do to stammer out one thing. "What in the world was that wind gust!?"

"I'd guess around forty-five miles an hour. They sure can come out of nowhere and knock you down if you aren't paying attention."

CHAPTER 5:

HEAT ADVISORY- HE'S WEARING THAT HAT AGAIN

My alarm went off extra early the next morning as I planned to have time for reading my Bible. Something I had not done as often as I had hoped in the last week. In spending time in the Word, I felt peace over my relationships and current place in life. While I didn't consider things completely over with Jett forever, they definitely were at least for the time being, and that had to be okay. I had no means to leave there and find another rental somewhere else. Heck, until I could get my first paycheck, I couldn't even fill my car up with gas.

I cringed as I took off the large bandage I had earned last night at Jett's house, worried that my small, but centrally located wound wouldn't be ready to go au natural. To my horror, it wasn't. I couldn't stand the thought of wearing this on air, so I dug through my personal supplies and located the smallest bandage I could find and decided I would risk the social faux pas and don it over the weekend so it could heal. It didn't quite do the trick, however, but it *almost* wasn't noticeable if I really played up my eye makeup. Sigh. It was days like that when I understood the appeal of bangs. If only cutting my hair short wouldn't send it straight upward.

On that day's agenda, before going to the station to watch a few older clips, it was imperative that I got a few groceries. But first, I really needed some coffee, so off to the Rusted Mug I went. The bell above the door didn't even need to chime that morning, because the moment I walked in, Carolina cheered with glee.

"Well, if it isn't our own Big Horn weather girl!" The coffee shop was bustling with a weekend crowd and a few people clapped. While I always tried to look somewhat presentable, that day I wasn't ready for a crowd. I sheepishly waved at a few folks who were sipping foamy lattes and eating scones and walked faster up to the register.

"Thank you for the entrance," I whispered, secretly hoping she didn't make a habit out of that.

"I had no idea you were our new weather girl. I think that's great. Plus, I just went out with your boss Nick Taylor last night." She winked.

"Ahh, so you're the girl he had to convince for a year to go out with him? How was roller skating?" She handed me a tall black Arabica coffee, and I took a sip, letting the flavorful tones hit my senses.

"It was a disaster. He was so nervous, so he ate too much spaghetti and *then* we went skating. Let's just say it wasn't *if* he was going to toss his cookies, but *when*—you catch my drift?" She was in high spirits while retelling the story, and I had the feeling she really liked him anyway.

"Will there be a second date?" I leaned in on the counter as we spoke.

"Girl, between you and me, I've wanted to marry this guy since the third grade." Carolina looked like she had hearts in her eyes.

"So, why did it take you so long to go out with him?"

"Here's the thing about Nick: He *thinks* he's been in here wooing me for a year, right? In reality, he's been quietly ordering coffees and immediately leaving for a year. Once, he left before I even made the coffee! He gets painfully nervous around me, and I absolutely love it. My personality is strong, like my coffee," Carolina gave me a wink at her pun, "and I eat that stuff up. The girls and I had a betting pool for the date he would finally ask. They all lost, because I finally had to ask him out last week just because I couldn't take it anymore."

"I can't wait to see you together. I'm so happy for you two." What a cute pair they would make.

"Thank you, girly. I'm going to ask him to be my boyfriend tonight when he takes me to the movies, because otherwise, I might not get a ring until 2045. Better just get ahead of the equation here." I gave her a five-dollar bill for my coffee and when she handed me the change, I put it in her tip jar.

"Put this toward the wedding fund." I winked back and we both had a giggle. Thanking her, I left and headed back to my rental to get my car, and left for the grocery store, coffee in tow.

Prices there were astronomically higher for groceries than what I was used to, but being as remote as it was, it didn't shock me. The real problem lay in the lack of options. While they didn't have more than one brand of something to choose, they did have all the makings for meals. I got a box of pancake mix, stuff for chicken Caesar salads, spaghetti, and popcorn. But when I reached the coffee section, I couldn't find anything that compared to the brew that Carolina had. Still, buying a basic blend, as I didn't think my paycheck could support such an expensive daily habit, I decided I would treat myself to coffee and Carolina's budding friendship a few days a week.

Pushing my cart to the checkout line, I walked past the store's bakery and caught a whiff of the delectable treats they were putting out. A lovely selection of donuts, cakes and pies made my mouth water. I was mid-sniff when a familiar voice came up behind me.

"You sure do have a thing for sweets, don't ya? I just can't figure out where you put it." I turned to find the most aggravating man on the planet looking me up and down. I returned the favor.

"And I don't know where you put your manners, speaking to me like that." Okay, not my best comeback, but it was better than staying silent. He let out a low whistle.

"Careful, darlin'. I may not have a brain, but I do have a heart. And you're breaking it." He laughed, which admittedly I found incredibly gorgeous, and walked away.

"That's it?" The words were out of my mouth faster than I could realize. Was I *asking* him to stay? He spun back around on his heels.

"That's it." He turned again as he was carrying a jug of milk to the self-checkout. What was that guy's *problem?* How could that guy rock my world so much and then just walk away?

It infuriated me. My thoughts quickly reverted to Jett, but I shooed them away. I was incredibly hurt that Jett ended things with me, but unlike that guy, I couldn't see the future. God would work things out for the good of His glory, and I would remain faithful to that.

Once I grabbed a few things of fruit, I made my way to the check stand, paid, and left. The parking lot was full to the brim, being a weekend and all, I was guessing, but since it was also the first time I'd been there, I couldn't say for a fact that people didn't come there to hang out. I meant, what else was there to do in a place like that? I giggled at the thought, since it was likely my largest excursion that weekend, and it was only Saturday morning.

Later that morning, I went into the station. Nick had a handful of tapes out, with one in the player loaded. "All you have to do is press play. There are even some apples and chips in the break room. Just lock up behind you, will ya? I better get going."

"Have fun on your date." Nick spun around and looked at me quizzically.

"How did you know I have a date?" I held up my paper coffee cup that had *Rustic Mug* in bold font.

"Was just in there for a refill about five minutes ago. You got this in the bag, Nick." I wasn't sure how he would take the hint, as Carolina said he was very introspective and cautious about dating, which I admired. Choosing a life partner is a big deal. But these two had apparently been in love since they were children, and if I had to guess, I'd pinpoint him to be around thirty. It was okay to rev up the engine a little and move things along. He tilted his head at me like a puppy dog that you'd just given a math equation to.

"Thank you, Hailey, for the very unexpected boost. I think I'll ask Carolina to be my girlfriend."

"More like, wife." I mumbled under my breath, thinking he had left the building.

"Really?" Nick held his hand to his chin pensively. "Do you think she would say yes? I mean, that's been the ultimate goal my whole life: marry Carolina." He made a banner in the air with his hands. I turned my body in the chair to him.

"So, what's the hold up, Nick? I don't mean to overstep my bounds here as I don't know either of you, but why the glacial pace?" Nick shrugged his shoulders.

"I think the same as everybody else; I don't want to get hurt." I understood that, being recently wounded by my own person whom I thought I would be together with forever. If Jett didn't come around, and I had to do that all over. I didn't know how that would look. "Alright, need anything else? I'm outta here."

"Nope, I'm good. See you Monday." I waved him off, as I locked the door behind him. There were no news programs on the weekends, as they had a hard enough time keeping news for the weekdays, I was guessing. A weekend at least meant two full days of happenings that could spread out over the next five if need be.

As I watched the tapes, it was clear the town reported quite a bit on high school sports. I learned all about a handful of triple-letter varsity athletes and where they picked for college. While the news wasn't incredibly exciting, some of it really warmed my heart. It was a small, tight knit community that cared for their people, and I admired that. The news segments with Donny Gray were about as funny as Jett's parents said; the first one I watched, Donny was explaining the front of his knee that had an arthritic joint which *always* flared up right before moisture. I had a good laugh, but not at his expense. He was a very charismatic figure, and I could see why they kept him around despite no real weather reporting or knowledge on how to get the reports himself. Especially in the days of smart phones; Why didn't he just download a weather app and report from there? It was a mystery but also added to the flavor of the town that I was almost starting to enjoy. Almost.

I watched six tapes before calling it a day and heading back home. The coffee had given me jitters, and I was in need of a good meal. I went home and made a box of macaroni that I'd picked up at the store, curling up on the couch with the warm bowl. The creaminess of the cheese always comforted me and brought back memories of my childhood; though there were better meals with higher quality ingredients, there were none as comforting for me. As I ate, I talked to.

"Why am I here, Lord? Has Jett given up on me? Was I with Jett for the right reasons?" Through introspection and prayer, I felt God nudge me with the realization of what a control freak I was. Constantly, in every situation, I was always trying to guide the tide, under the guise of improvement, perfection, or higher standards. But really, I was running from fear, grief and loneliness. Though I was ashamed to admit it, I was not with Jett for love. He fit into my perfect plan that I concocted in my head. Sure, I liked Jett a lot, but if I hadn't fully given control of my life to God, how could I commit to anything? It had to end right then. I would never find peace in my life until I handed over the reins to Him. I didn't know how to say it, so I just started to pray.

Lord, whatever is Your will, I pray it will be. Please take away my control freak-ness. I can't do it on my own anymore, nor did you ever expect me to. I've been running for so long, and now I am running into Your arms, Lord. Take this pain away and guide me to where You want me to be. I believe, for something much greater than I can see right now, You wanted me in Wyoming. I'm here Lord, waiting for direction.

After sitting in silence with God for the rest of the afternoon, I felt grounded. Relaxed and peaceful. His work was so much greater than anything I could ever do in my own life. And right then, though I decided I wouldn't drive to visit Jett's family every single day, I wanted to put my slighted and hurt feelings aside and talk to someone who was dear to me. I sent Cindy a text, telling her I wouldn't be by today, but that I was thinking about her. She didn't reply, but given her energy levels were all over the board, I wasn't surprised.

It was just past six, and I was looking to the week ahead. I pulled out the phone number Nick gave me for the cameraman, Colt, and punched the numbers into my phone. A gruff voice answered on the other line, but the connection sounded choppy, and all I could hear was a bunch of cows mooing.

"Hi, Colt? This is Hailey Sinclair. I'm the new meteorologist at Big Horn News."

"The what? I didn't catch that." Colt was almost yelling over the mooing by then, and I regretted my call instantly.

"Meteorologist," I said again, firmly, but I just heard mooing. Finally, I used the term that everyone seemed to prefer around those parts: "Weather girl."

"Ahh. That's right, Nick had texted me about you. Okay, then."

"Anyway, I was wondering if there was a time on Monday we could get together once you're done with your cattle move." I prayed that was the right term, as I couldn't recall how Nick had described it. With a loud sound of a door closing, the mooing stopped.

"I'm free all day Monday." His voice reminded me of someone, but I couldn't think of who.

"Great. How about eight in the morning? I have a lot of story ideas, and it sounds like you and I will be on assignment together for them, so I'd like to devise a plan if we could and. . ."

"Should I be taking notes?"

"Excuse me?"

"I just am not sure if there's going to be a quiz later." Well, clearly we were off to a great start.

"I suppose I've caught you at a bad time," I said.

"This is as good a time as any, ma'am." *Ma'am?* Was there a worse thing to refer to a woman as than ma'am?

"Then I suppose it's always a bad time. I'll see you at the station on Monday at eight sharp. Don't be late." I hung up. I felt like I needed to catch my breath. *What is with the men out here? And why do they tick me off so much? Yes, I do have a plan, and people can get used to it. And I have things to say. Wait. Is God giving me an opportunity to give up my power-hungry ways, and I'm already failing?* I put my head in my hands. *Lord, I pray for this relationship with the cameraman. It's essential that we get along, at least on a tolerable level.* Since I'd gotten all the things done I needed to, there was just one other possibility for my weekend that involved dough, cinnamon, and all things sparkle.

I was *almost* disappointed to arrive at Georgianna's diner and not see a rude cowboy sitting on a barstool, but that feeling was outweighed with relief. "Heya, sweet cheeks. I saw you on the news last night. Nice to see someone with beauty and brains on our local news. Did you come here for the job or somethin'? Or are you like me and movin' here for a cowboy?"

"Well, sort of the latter, but he isn't a cowboy, not really, anyway." Georgianna looked at me like that was the most interesting thing she'd ever heard. I instinctively checked my texts to see if Cindy had ever responded, which she hadn't.

"Girl, sit right down here and tell me the whole story while I plate some fresh rolls, and I promise you'll get the best one of the batch if you don't leave anything out. Not one to refuse such a good offer, I took a seat at the furthest end of the diner bar on a firm, white sparkle seat, and told her the whole story.

"Where should I begin?" Talking about myself was hard. A hurdle I never found the strength to get past since my mother died, and that night, with such a warm ear to talk to, I felt myself getting emotional right off the bat. "My mother died when I was seven."

Georgianna put her hand over mine for a glimpse of time, shaking her head. "Bless your heart." I told her the rest of my story, and how I'd grown extraordinarily attached to Jett's mother, dated for all the wrong reasons, and my fixation on the idea of Dana Summers, going so far as to become a meteorologist.

"Do you enjoy the work?" she asked.

"You know what's funny?" I took a bite of the cinnamon roll while I pondered. "I've never once thought about that until just now. But, I suppose it's all I've ever known, and I can't imagine myself doing anything else."

People shuffled in and out all night, and I didn't pay a lick of attention to anyone, nor did they to me. It was really nice to be engrossed in conversation with another woman my age. It had been so long since I made any real friendships. I certainly had none at school.

"Your faith is there, Hailey. God put you here in this rinky dink town for a reason. I know sometimes we look around us and think, 'God, you really have a sense of humor cuz I know this ain't right,' but for another person, like myself? Girl, this place is an answer to a lifetime of prayers. If it ain't for that husband of mine finding me in some backwoods hoe down overlookin' a swamp, complete with a man holding a pitchfork waitin' for some alligator to jump out and give him a crusty look, I can't tell you where I'd be today."

As our conversation came to a natural close, I looked over at my shoulder. The place was hopping with locals of all ages, but Georgianna had two teenage women helping her serve that night, so she could focus on the product, but she had been very engrossed in our conversation all night. I thanked her for such a lovely conversation and the sugary sweet, that she was right—had to be the best of the batch—and got up. Looking over the counter, she had only three cinnamon rolls left.

"Did you sell through all fifty of those already?"

Georgianna gave me a radiant smile. "God is good."

"And those cinnamon rolls are heaven sent." She came around the corner and gave me a hug. Georgianna was right. While my situation might not have been my dream come true, there was more to the journey than myself. God wanted me there right at that moment, and there I was.

When Monday morning rolled around, I discovered I hadn't needed to set my alarm clock. The roosters picked up all the slack around there. Waking up to a fresh scream with the sunrise, while on a farm, that you were warned about in advance, and walking out to a breakfast buffet complete with fresh squeezed orange juice was one thing. Waking up to a surprise scream that you were *not* warned about at sunrise, in a new area with no food prepared nor coffee nor juice, was quite another experience. After I worked through the shock and realized I was better off getting up a few minutes early than trying to fall back asleep, I slid out of my covers and decided there would be enough time that morning to properly do my hair and makeup.

I drove down to the station, though it was only four blocks from my house, so that I wouldn't need to ride with Colt. I could already tell that it was going to be a weird day by how it started, but somehow, I knew that the upcoming experience would top it.

It was 8:02 a.m. when a pickup truck with tinted windows pulled into the lot. Nicer than I had expected for such a jerk, a newer, boxier style—but still, not very timely. I purposely was looking down at my notes when he walked up so that I could shade him. "Look who decided to show up." And then I felt his presence. A familiar, aggravating, annoying presence of a man who irritated every nerve in my body for no reason. I peeked up to the gorgeous man from the diner and the grocery store, with his arms crossed and giving me the biggest grin I'd ever seen.

"Colt Wilder?" It couldn't be. This was the man I had to work with?

"Hailey Sinclair." He didn't ask, but instead, tipped his hat. His *cowboy hat.* Suddenly, I felt like it was almost a joke. "Ready to get all *cowboy?*" Ugh, I knew it! He was teasing me. I felt piping hot as my blood boiled through my veins. What is it about that guy? Other than his gorgeous looks, I couldn't help but want to strangle him.

"Look," I started out, then realizing that moment might be another opportunity given by our great Lord to stop being a control freak, I took a breath, "We have an assignment; let's get it done. I'll follow you there." I handed him a slip about the ranger station roof and started walking to my car.

"That's fine, but you'll need 4WD to get there. You got that? Oh, and the road is blown out halfway up. You'll need to cross a river, and it might be high with all that snow runoff. But if you want to ride with me, you can." I exhaled a deep breath and refrained from stomping into the ground.

"Fine. But I pick the music." He let out a low whistle and walked to the passenger side of the truck, opening the door for me. I was not used to the gesture. Though Jett was a gentleman, I'd never had a man open a car door for me. "Well, aren't you a peach?" I said, half sarcastically. "Thank you," I stammered out, which took all of my strength to do once I was in the truck. He waited until I was buckled before closing the door.

"You're welcome." His square jawline was chiseled, and I noticed how muscular his neck looked under his layers of shirt.

"He must work out," I whispered to myself, matter of factly. As we started driving to the station, I realized there was no way my car could have even imagined taking those roads, and I definitely, one hundred and fifty percent wore the wrong shoes. After a long and bumpy road, we finally arrived. "Is there any way you can pull the truck right up to that concrete pad? I chose the wrong footwear for this assignment." It looked like he was thinking for a minute, but ultimately, shook his head.

"No can do. That says, 'No Parking.' Right there. Do you see the sign? You wouldn't want me to *break the law* now, would you?"

"I—no—but-," I tried to stammer out a way to convince him, but he'd already exited the vehicle and shut his door. I saw him walking around to my side again, and I was about to suck it up and walk when I unbuckled my seatbelt. The door swung open, and he reached inside, picking me up like I was weightless and carrying me like he'd just rescued me from a burning building, then placing me onto the concrete pad. It all happened so quickly that I was standing on my feet before he was gone again, off to fetch the camera, presumably. I couldn't deny that it was helpful, but the chances of him getting a parking ticket in the middle of nowhere seemed slim to none, as well.

Colt returned in a flash with a camera slung over his shoulder, a tripod in one hand and a microphone in the other. I reached, grabbing the official Big Horn News microphone and thanked him. I rehearsed the story I prepared the day before while he set up. Before he got finished, the clouds started to roll in. "Oh no," I said, instinctively, at the weather. I knew we were going to get some showers that day, but I had hoped they would hold off until the afternoon. I wasn't afraid of getting wet, but being a curly haired girl, it would have been easier if I didn't.

"Don't tell me the weather girl didn't know we were going to have rain showers this morning?" His smart attitude had been getting on my nerves since I first met him, but he was right. I should've known it. I checked my forecast notes. Ugh!

"No, I knew. I just somehow transposed today and tomorrow morning. Geez, I hope I didn't say it backwards on Friday like I wrote it down here."

"You sure did." A pit fell in my stomach. "But don't worry. There isn't a soul in this town watching the news for the weather. Nothing personal—they are tuning in for the beautiful woman giving the weather all right, but things change out here on a dime. Your fancy weather programs are going to say one thing, and a minute later, they will be upside down opposite. That is how it's always been and always will be. For some reason, it's impossible to predict it in our pocket of the Rockies." His words gave me comfort, though I would never tell him that, but the logic wasn't making sense in my head. I supposed there was the possibility of weather dissipating over the mountain ranges, but I decided I would consult the issue with my college professor later that day.

"So, are you saying that you watched the news on Friday? During your big cow move?"

"Cattle drive."

"During your cattle drive—you pulled out a phone to live stream?"

"Nah, I was home by then. They aren't my cows. They are my brother's; I just help him from time to time. Managed to escape having my butt glued to a saddle for four days this time and was able to follow the cows in my truck. Could only drive one mile an hour, but so worth it to be home at night. And I was able to catch your very interesting comment about how cowboy it is here." He hid his smirk behind the camera as he continued to set up, and I felt my face blush three shades. "Okay, I'm all set up. Something tells me you're ready to start talking." For once, he was right. I just needed a minute to refocus my lines. I held my hand up in a gesture to give me a minute while I read over my notes once more, perfecting a few tricky words I had back-to-back, and made sure to take my sweet time. After several minutes, I felt confident I could read them by memory.

"Good day, Big Horn Wyoming. This is Dana Summers reporting from—" Oh my word. What childhood memory crevasse did I just pull that from? "Uh—sorry. Cut. Let's rewind the tape, please." Thankfully, he didn't comment on my monumental screw up and did as I had asked. He had *some* sense to give me grace at a time of need, at least. I pulled myself together, remembering fondly when I was ten how I used to impersonate Dana's stories. There was one when she visited a hurricane spot that I had memorized. I'm thanking the Lord and praying that that mistake didn't happen on air, when Colt said he was ready to go. Taking a deep breath, I started again.

"Good evening, Big Horn Wyoming. This is Hailey Sinclair reporting from the Rimrock Ranger Station." I paused, giving Colt time to cut the clip after my opening, as we were going to move the frame to the side of the building afterward . He did, and I walked around the back of the building, my high heels letting everyone know within a 100-yard radius that I actually believed those shoes would be a good idea.

After we were done shooting, I was really pleased with how professional the morning was. It was nearly eleven, and my stomach let me know it was time to eat. As we drove back down the mountain, I was taking inventory of what food options I had at home and already dressing the Caesar salad in my head when his phone rang. It sounded like something bad had happened to the caller, and then Colt told him he had an idea, and he'd be right over. The worst part was, he took a turn in whatever direction this place was, and it was going in the opposite direction of the station.

"Hi, almost complete stranger? Are you luring me into the woods to kill me, or can we get back to the station now?"

"Just trust me on this. I have an idea for a story."

"Oh yeah?" I came off a little snarkier than I intended, but he seemed to like it, judging by his quick smile.

"Yeah. A story so good, you'd probably win a daytime Emmy for it." I knew he was too sarcastic to mean that, but I was intrigued, nonetheless. After all, the work I did there mattered.

"So, tell me, then."

"There's a rancher, Sam Marshall, about thirty minutes that way, out on the plains, that had pretty bad hail damage yesterday. But, uh, he's got a really angry goat. He's been cross eyed since birth. Like this animal is out for blood, right? A small old barn straight up collapsed onto the goat, and that sucker not only lived, but he's angrier than ever. I think this could be a really fun story for our community. What do you say?"

"You had me at 'angry goat'," I smiled, agreeing that it sounded like a fun story.

"That's my girl." I felt my cheeks redden as soon as Colt spoke the words, and he immediately looked away, as if he wasn't intending to say them. He was looking out the driver's side window, so I took the chance to steal a look at his masculine hands on the steering wheel. He really was a rugged cowboy. I had never been around a man that manly before, and I couldn't deny that I liked it.

We arrived at the ranch half past noon, and Colt rolled his window down to chat with the rancher. "Just go on and park right over there, by the barn. But watch out for rattlers. I've been dang near hoping one would get mean ole' Filbert, but last week, I kid you not, he had one of them doggone rattlers in his mouth. I don't got one of those smartphones with the picture taker on it, but if I did, I suppose that might make some national news or be on one of those cuckoo clock videos my granddaughters are all about."

"I reckon you're right about that, Sam. Thanks for having us. Where is Filbert now? Want to make sure I don't enter into his path." The way the men spoke about that goat made me chuckle. The only goats I'd ever been around were baby goats at a farmers market near my college campus. One of the cheesemakers brought it by to help sell the product, and boy was that a hit. It was the most darling little creature I'd ever seen.

"Hoo boy! There he is. I better get!" Sam took off running in a way I'd never seen. He had both arms out like a scarecrow and was hollering all the way into his barn. I'd estimated him to be in his sixties, but he ran like he was in his nineties.

"Does he need help?" I asked Colt, who'd been steadily watching the whole thing from the safety of the truck, going as far as to roll the window back up.

"Probably, but we're about to need more help than him, if we're lucky."

"What do you mean, 'if we're lucky'?"

"Trust me, *this* is going to be a story." Colt was laughing under his breath, thinking I couldn't tell, and though I was confused, for some reason I did trust him. The goat looked small from where I sat, and awfully precious. Filbert stood there, innocently wearing a knitted pale green sweater. I smirked at the thought of grown men being afraid of anything in a *sweater.* He did have two sets of little Billy goat horns on his head, pointed in different directions, like a little devil. Filbert ran to the barn but stopped at the closed door. Maybe he just wanted to play? Goats could be playful, right? I didn't see why not. Colt moved the truck over to right in front of the barn and hopped into his truck bed as soon as he got out of the truck. He angled the camera inside the truck bed, like we were on a high-speed chase and needed to get away on the fly.

"All set, Hailey. Do you know what you're going to say?"

"I was thinking I'd just talk about the goat and the barn collapsing. Maybe we could get a clip of the goat being alive, you know, so people know he's okay? I would hate to have people worry that he's not."

"Trust me, no one will be losing sleep about Filbert when something finally gets him. Don't worry about Filly. I think Sam's got him tied up now. Okay, I'm going to start rolling in three. . .two. . .one. . ."

"Good day, Big Horn Wyoming. This is Hailey Sinclair reporting from Sam Marshall's ranch, about 30 miles west of Big Horn." I paused, and Colt took the cue and shifted the angle, to which I was then standing next to the collapsed barn, instead of in front of it on camera. "Sam experienced something yesterday that no rancher would ever want to go through: Due to severe hail damage, this barn to my left came crumbling down. And inside of the barn, was his precious goat, Filbert." A rattle off camera made my ear perk up, but I knew Sam was supposed to come over for an on-camera interview, so I assumed it was him, and I went on. "Sam reported that the hail stones were as large as golf balls, and when they came pelting from the sky, they hit an already weakened part of his barn's roofline. One that had already survived an ice dam this past winter, but he never imagined it would be hail that would take it out." Colt gave me a thumbs up as I paused, and he shifted the camera once more. This time, I wasn't sure what angle he was shooting, as since the barn was then out of the frame completely. He gave a finger countdown, and I began again.

"But while tragedy wiped out a treasured structure on his ranch—the barn that his father built with his own two hands in the early 1920's—a miracle was still inside, alive and well. Filbert, Sam Marshall's goat, had miraculously survived the collapse." A scraping noise was getting louder, and Colt's eyes grew wide, while he zoomed his camera lens on something to the right of me. I turned my head and screamed in horror, as Filbert had locked eyes on me, head down and horns out—and he was coming my way. I threw the microphone down, trying to break into a run, but the ground was soggy, and I was in high heels. It was inevitable that I would end up in a face plant at some part of the day, but I was hoping to hold off for a while. I managed to get back to the truck with only dirt on my knees, but the door was locked.

"Colt! Can you help me here?" I stood on the running boards and tried to shoo the goat away, but he was rabid. The sweater didn't look so cute all of a sudden. It looked like it needed to be a straitjacket instead. While Colt fumbled for his truck keys, saying something about how the doors automatically lock, I couldn't entirely hear him over his laughter. I grabbed one of my heels, thinking the point would ward the goat off, when Sam whistled loudly at Filbert.

"Sorry, guys. I got a bucket of food for him. This should do the trick." Filbert bit the heel of my shoe, running off with it towards Sam. Finally, the truck doors unlocked, and I was able to climb inside, but at a loss for words for what had just happened. Colt was keeled over laughing, and my pulse felt like my heart might just beat out of my chest. That was terrifying. I took back everything nice I thought about the goat—he was not playful or just being friendly. He wanted blood to be shed. Colt hopped out of his truck bed, coming over to my side, and opened the door.

"Are you okay, Hailey?" He was trying not to laugh, but clearly, not hard enough.

"I thought you said he was tied up?" I asked him, arms crossed, covered in dirt, hair messy, and missing a shoe. It didn't help that half of my toenail polish was chipped off or just MIA in general.

"Did I say that?"

Colt infuriated me. I was fuming mad. Colt thought he had to worry about Filbert, but it was about to be me coming after him. I gave him *the look,* and he took off for the other side of his truck. But when I jumped back out of the truck, wearing one high heel, the height misalignment threw me off, and I fell for real. Into the mud. Face first. I tried to get up fast, so maybe no one would notice I was completely covered in mud head to toe, but Colt was back in his truck bed with the camera pointed at me.

"Would you be angry if I told you I never turned the camera off?" I quietly asked the Lord if screaming would help in that situation. Taking a deep breath, I refocused my heart on what was right, and honest, and true, as I started to catch a whiff of whatever it was that my bare foot was seeped in. *Manure.*

"Colt. . .Turn. The. Camera. Off." He knew I meant business and nodded his head.

"Roger that. It's off."

"Now what?" I asked him, expecting him to come up with a solution since he got me into that mess. Who locks the doors while standing in the back of their truck?

"Ratings gold. I smell an Emmy in your future."

"That's not what you smell." I was on the verge of tears, and my voice cracked as I spoke.

"Yeah, I think there's a hose around here somewhere."

CHAPTER 6:
WINDS OF AWKWARD CHANGE

After a very literal hose down, with what felt like a tool from a fire truck, Sam Marshall's wife had done a swell job helping me clean up. She even gave me a change of clothes to wear back home. "I know you'll be swimming in these, Hailey, as I haven't been your size since I was a child. But they are clean and comfortable. You're welcome to keep them."

Looking down at my outfit of patchwork sweats, slippers, and an oversized cat sweater, I was just thrilled to be out of the muddy clothes. "Thank you so much for helping me in my time of need, Dottie. That's some goat you got out there." Being clean and warm, I was already in better spirits.

"That reminds me. While you were changing, Sam was able to recover your shoe." She handed me back my high heel that had since been cleaned up and surprisingly, wasn't missing a bite out of it anywhere.

Dottie led me out to the front porch where Colt was waiting for me. "She'll be alright, just tread lightly. Poor thing has been through a lot. And she might need a tetanus shot."

Colt came to my side, leading me by the arm for the first few steps like I was being discharged from the hospital. "Woah, there. I can still walk. Just unlock your truck doors this time."

"Already unlocked, darlin'."

"Don't darlin' me, Colt." Colt smiled. Clearly, he was egged on by the subtle rejection but quickly walked ahead and opened the truck door for me.

"Thank you," I said politely as I climbed into the passenger seat, with him closing the door behind me.

"Don't forget this, Colt." Sam held up a bag of my clothes, and Colt ran over to grab it. He tipped his hat and shared a few quick words with them, before jogging back to the truck. I checked my watch; I had to report back to the station in three hours, and Colt still had to edit that video for later that night. We were in a bit of a time crunch, not to mention I was starving. As he climbed into the truck, I refused to look at him.

"You gotta admit, that was absolutely hilarious." He busted up again, pulling out his phone to show me a few stills he took from the camera footage. "I meant it, Hailey. This is about to pop off when we share it later." He reached over to show a photo of me mid-run, with the look of maximum panic washed over my face as Filbert chased me. I smirked, holding back my laughter as he swiped to the next one, where I was standing on his truck running boards, holding out the spike of my high-heel shoe. The last swipe revealed me covered in mud, giving a look so angry, I put Filbert to shame. Colt was right; this was absolutely hilarious material, but I didn't want to put this on television.

"There's no way this story goes live, Colt." I broke the news after we pulled back on the two-lane highway, heading back to Big Horn. He almost came to a complete stop with the look of shock on his face.

"And why wouldn't we share this? The people will eat this up, Hailey! I've already posted a sneak peek on the Big Horn News ViralVideo channel. It's got nearly a thousand views, Hailey—there's not even 1,000 people who watch the nightly news! This is a great sign!"

"You WHAT? This is out there? Me making a fool of myself? Dana Summers would never—," I cut that short. Colt did not need to know anything about my idealization of her career, and the one I wanted to model my own after.

"You sure do like Dana Summers, huh? I get it now. You've got that whole classy vibe thing going on just like her."

"Um, thank you?"

"You're welcome." I grudgingly looked at Colt when he smiled and saw not only did his teeth sparkle, but his eyes, too. He was annoyingly gorgeous—but everything about him seemed to irritate my very being.

"Look, I think it's great that this clip could bring the station attention; I just don't think it's right for my career, is all."

"Hailey," Colt pulled over on the side of the road and turned to me, "I would never do anything to put you in a bad light or compromise your future. I just want you to trust me on this. I can edit the heck out of this video and will keep the funniest parts for just you and me, but please give me your blessing to use the rest of it for your fame and glory. It will be so good that Dana Summers will wish she'd thought of it first." He spoke so honestly and earnestly that I felt my fears melt away.

"Okay, fine. But let me see the video first. I reserve the right to approve it first."

"Deal." He looked into my eyes for a moment longer before merging back onto the road. "We've got a little bit of a drive. Tell me about this boyfriend of yours. You think I could take him?" He clearly thought he was the funniest guy alive, but I felt gutted thinking of Jett with his mom right then. Whether or not I was with him for the right reasons, I still cared deeply for him and would marry him the next day if he asked.

"Your music taste is worse than I expected." I turned up the dial to drown out the questions, leaving it on some 90's pop song.

"And you're deflecting. Trouble in paradise?"

"This coming from the guy who thinks I talk too much?"

"I never said it was a bad thing."

"Whatever. I don't really want to talk about Jett right now is all." I wrestled with my mind after I accidentally slipped his name into the mix. It was a very small town, and no doubt, both guys knew each other. Though, Colt was at least a few years older than us.

"Jett Dawson?" He straightened in his seat, and I could swear his voice dropped an octane.

"The one and only."

"Nice family. Don't know him personally or anything. But my little sister had the biggest crush on him all through high school, so I feel like I know everything about him."

"Is that so?" I was intrigued to hear it, as Jett said he didn't really date in high school, but for some reason that felt gossipy and like I was learning something I had no business hearing. "In that case, you should know that his mom, Cindy, has got a really bad deal going on right now with cancer. That's why I'm here."

"I am so sick of cancer." Colt shook his head. "Took my dad last year. But now he's living it up with the Lord. Right before he died, his mind was on its way out. He couldn't recognize the people in his room, but one morning he sat up and looked me straight in the eye and said my name, and that he had something to tell me."

"Well, what did he say?"

Colt smiled, letting the story build up. "He leans in and says, 'Colt, I've got my bags packed, and a one-way ticket to Heaven. Jesus is calling my name. But don't worry, by the time you get there, I'll have perfected my harp solo, and I'll play it for you.' So, I asked him, what song are you going to learn? And without any hesitation or thought, he says, 'It Is Well with My Soul.' He died a few minutes later, right there. When I leave later that day, I get in my truck and guess what song is on the radio? I felt like God was extending me comfort in that very moment with the song."

"That's a beautiful story, Colt. I'm sorry you lost your dad. I lost my mom to it when I was a kid." Colt briefly extended his hand out, as if he was going to place it on mine but pulled back at the last minute.

"I'm sorry to hear that. And now you're watching the battle of another person in your life that I'm sure means a lot to you." I felt like I'd hijacked the story about his dad and made it about me.

"I don't mean to take the focus off of your story."

"You didn't. There's room for both of us, Hailey." Something about Colt's words were so new and refreshing to me. I didn't want to compare Jett and Colt, because at the end of the day, Jett had been my long-time boyfriend and Colt my one day colleague, but I'd never felt like I could share my grievances with Jett. Especially not at that time since he was battling something so horrible in his own family. It was nice to have someone to talk to whom I felt really heard me. But it wasn't a moment later he did something to irk me royally once again.

"I got another story: There's a local duck pond, right? Well, there is a stunning gazebo that I've always thought would make the perfect backdrop for a story. It's where couples like to take pictures. Prom, engagement—heck, even weddings —

lots of small town events happen at this scenic pond. And right now, it's currently covered in a colorful flower garland because someone just got married there." It did sound quite beautiful, and while I was intrigued, I didn't quite have the capacity right then to plan another story. I just needed to get a shower.

"No offence, Colt—but let's get through today before we plan another outing. Okay?"

"Fair enough." Nothing deterred Colt's bright smile, which made me aggravated. Was he capable of being calm, or was he always sunshine? We drove the rest of the way with the radio cranked up on an admittedly a worse selection than what he had originally. When we reached the station, my stomach growled. "Want to grab a bite to eat? We still have a few hours before we need to report back."

"Easy for you to say; you're not going to be on camera in a few hours. I better get going." I slid out of his truck, the slippers on my feet doing little to soften the step.

"There you go, breaking my heart again."

"And there you go, driving me nuts again. What is with you, Colt, that irritates my every last nerve?" I stared at him blankly, realizing I'd gone too far, too soon with someone I didn't even know. But I couldn't take it back. *Lord, please help me with my controlling temper once again.*

Much to my chagrin, Colt didn't respond in a timely manner, so I shut the truck door and quickly got in my car and drove the few blocks to my rental. Shutting the door behind me, I almost felt choked up from what I had said. Why was I so mean?

A long, hot shower was double time as a prayer session as I washed all of the mud and goat out of my long golden curls. I knew I'd been hurt from the loss of my mother, but I started to notice a pattern. Aside from Jett, I'd pushed everyone away in my life, including that of my father. And with Jett—did we even truly know each other? I wasn't sure. I meant, I knew things about him. I knew his family. I felt his passion for everything he enjoyed—playing frisbee with his friends, studying, and worshipping the Lord. He was a comfortable part of my life and suddenly, I wasn't quite ready to let that go just yet.

When I had my hair up in a towel, I fished my phone out of my purse and gave him a call. He answered on the fourth ring.

"Hey, Hailey." My heart leapt at his voice. He sounded in good spirits, at least an improvement from where he was the other night.

"Jett. Hi." Something in me felt. . .different. I wanted Jett more than I ever had. I was no longer complacent. Spending time with another man, albeit platonically, had proven that in leaps and bounds. Jett did nothing to annoy me. He never said anything rude or upsetting. He was a real gem of a guy, and of course, incredibly handsome, in an athletic, preppy way. "I was just thinking about you. Can we see each other tonight, after I get off work?"

"Only if you promise to not hit your head again on the railing." I ran my hands over my forehead that I smacked on the wood the past night. It was tender. I was just thankful it didn't break the skin. How would I have looked running from that goat while also wearing a large Band-aid on my forehead?

"To stay on the safe side, why don't we go out for just a little while? How about Georgianna's for dessert?" A long pause let me know that Jett was hesitant to leave his family. While I didn't blame him, I was hopeful that he could give me just an hour of his time.

"Okay."

Okay! He agreed. Why did I feel like I was forcing him away? *Never mind that right now.* We agreed to meet at seven and ended the call. The pep in my step was returning as I styled my hair, taking extra time to pick out a cute outfit to wear on air, given that Jett and his parents would be watching that night. I thought back to my message to Cindy; she still hadn't responded, not that she needed to, but I sent her another text on the fly to let her know I'd make sure Jett would be bringing her home a cinnamon roll that night.

Not a moment later, she put a heart on the message, but still no text reply. That was okay. She had millions of other things to be thinking about right then. Including how much I cared for her, so I sent that in a message, too.

After devouring lunch, brushing my teeth, and a final spritz of Jett's favorite vanilla scented perfume, I tore out of the house and headed to the station. I still had weather analyzing to do, and I needed to be there extra early to ensure that Colt didn't post anything heinous involving that goat.

Nancy, whom I hadn't seen since the day I interviewed for the job, was sitting at a large rounded desk inside the front doors of the station when I arrived. "Well, if it isn't our new meteorologist! I knew you'd get the job. And you're already doing wonderful!" She held out her arms to me and gave me a hug. Part of me wanted to know if she caught a whiff of any farm-related residue on me still, but her smile was bright, and I took that as a sign I'd successfully removed it all.

"Thank you, Nancy. I am happy to be here."

"So is everyone. I checked, asking each staffer individually. They all think you are very sharp and up to the task. Since I only work a few days a week, I had some serious catching up to do this morning." She winked at me, coyly. Leaning in, she lowered her tone, but not the volume. "Now, you should know that I'm a bit of a matchmaker and—."

"She's got a boyfriend, Nance." Colt strutted through the lobby just in time to interrupt our conversation, but for once, I was pleased he did. Nancy waited for him to walk to the other side of the studio and shut his office door, which he only completed the former. It was so obvious he was listening in on our conversation, so I made sure to give him exactly what he wanted.

"It's true. I'm madly in love with my boyfriend of three years." Her eyebrows raised so high I thought they would touch her hairline.

"Is that so?"

I wasn't sure how to handle her questioning me. What—did she not believe me? This woman knew absolutely zilch about me, yet had the audacity to second guess my relationship status? Sure, we might have been on a break right then, but that was neither here nor there. What could I possibly have said to this near perfect stranger, whom I could sense was extraordinarily connected in that tightly-knit town, to convince her otherwise?

"Yep." I tiptoed away from her skepticism and went to my office and closed the door. The rest of my free time was spent looking at the weather models and forecast for the upcoming week. With the ever-changing direction of the wind gusts, my mind was confused on how people actually made a forecast there at all.

"Knock knock," Colt said as he walked right into my office, no actual knock done.

"Speaking of *complicated*."

"What's that?" If I didn't already believe that guy was full of himself to the max and incapable of being emotionally wounded, I would have said he was truly hurt by my words earlier. As I contemplated some sort of apology, he interjected, "I have the goat goat video if you're ready to watch it."

"The goat *goat?*"

"Yeah, as in the 'greatest of all time' goat video."

"I see what you did there." With a dramatic eye roll, I hit the switch on my monitor to turn it off. Until I knew for sure about that storm, I didn't need anyone else accidentally catching wind of it.

Colt was right. My mind tried to grasp that the man who asked me to trust him *was* trustworthy, because the goat video was in fact, *gold.* "I love it," I whispered, closing my eyes so I wouldn't see or feel how attractive he was when he smiled. If only his personality could be exchanged for anyone else on earth. Well, maybe not *anyone,* as I couldn't see myself dating someone who liked to run marathons on holidays.

"I knew you would, Hailey." He winked.

"I'm pretty sure I didn't know I would." We both had a laugh, and I turned to walk away.

"Since I knocked this one out of the park—how about we go see a pond about a gazebo tomorrow? Say, ten in the morning?"

"Why so late—do you need to get your beauty sleep?" I razzed him.

"Nah, I just have something to do, that's all."

"Fine. If Nick likes this clip of the goat, that is, I suppose I'm up for seeing this scenic backdrop."

"I love the clip, Hailey." Nick came in from the hallway with a cup of coffee. "I think it's going to perform really well on our ViralVideo channel." He was grinning ear to ear, and while I wanted to ask him about his date with Carolina, I thought I'd wait until Colt wasn't in the room. Rather not have him think I'd gone soft all of the sudden.

"Alright, I guess the pond is on. But how in the world is it weather related?"

"There's a flock of ducks that relocate when they can sense a storm brewing. They are like the groundhogs of the weather. And they've been gone for an unusually long time."

Once we got through the nightly news, and I gave a very carefully-worded weather forecast, since they really did seem to change fast in that part of the Rockies, I gathered up the things and went to speak with Nick.

"Great job, Hailey. We're about to roll the goat segment here, but on ViralVideo, it's already gotten ten thousand views! That's viral in my book." Nick turned his laptop around to show me the stats. Wow, it really was gaining traction. "Oh, here it is." We both looked at the monitors as they rolled the clip. First, I was standing in front of the dilapidated barn. Unfortunately, my high heels were in the shot, which I didn't love. I really needed some better footwear for on-scene stories like that. The next clip, I was speaking in detail about what happened. Colt had zoomed into the hail damage, and by the time he zoomed out, Filbert had me in his crosshairs. One second he looked innocent, and the next, it looked like he was trying out to participate in the running of the bulls. The video skipped the part where I fell running away from him and jumped to an abbreviated clip of me asking Colt to unlock the truck doors and being covered in mud. It was all in good fun, and while I was expecting to hate it, I found it really enjoyable and despite it all, classy.

"That was great. What a fun clip," I remarked as Nick waited while Donny rolled it into a commercial break.. "And how was your weekend?" Nick stood, putting his arms in the air as if to show victory.

"She's the one!"

"Was there ever any doubt there?"

"Well, no. At least not for me. But she made her intentions clear last night, and we're on the same page."

"That's wonderful, Nick. Carolina seems like a great gal. I'm happy for you both. Well, I'm going to head out. I have a date of my own tonight."

I left the station, and when I looked back at the door as I was driving away, I swear I saw a silhouette of a cowboy looking back at me.

I changed into a casual but dressy ensemble; a loose fitted bright pink sweatshirt that was mildly cropped, with light wash jeans, white tennis shoes and big gold jewelry. My hair was half up, and I topped off the look with a soft pink gloss on my lips. There was something really churning in my mind that night, and for the first time in a long time—I was anxiously excited to see Jett.

Pulling into Georgianna's, I turned off my low beam headlights and waited for Jett while listening to the radio. I couldn't bear to go in by myself again lest I be known as the woman who gorged cinnamon rolls alone at night. When Jett finally pulled up a few minutes later, I turned off the car and nearly jumped into his arms.

"Hey." He seemed pleased to see me as I took him in for a deep hug, smothering him with affection.

"I missed you," I whispered into his ear, getting flirty with my glossy lips, but didn't kiss him, as we were broken up, after all.

"I missed you too, Hailey." My heart leapt as he spoke. We naturally took to holding hands as we walked into the diner, with my new friend Georgianna greeting us.

"Well, hey, look at you two kids. On a hot date I see. I better put you way over here."

When Jett started walking, Georgianna looked back at me and winked, gesturing for me to look behind me. Sure enough, Colt was in the diner. We locked eyes the moment I looked his way, and he stiffened in his seat. A woman sat across from him, and I didn't like how that made me feel. I cringed as Jett took the booth seat on the left, meaning I would be facing Colt from across the diner. But maybe that was a good thing, so I could see what everyone was up to that night. As Georgianna took our order: two cinnamon rolls and two large hot chocolates with extra whipped cream, she went to prepare them, and Jett started laughing.

"I never eat like this. Better just schedule a dentist visit right now." He pulled out his phone, pretending to look up the phone number before putting it away quickly. I couldn't help but feel he was just checking to see if his parents had messaged him and felt so bad that he was going through this.

"It's okay, just this once," I whispered, reaching out for his hands and meaning so much more than splurging on dessert. It was okay that he would be gone for just a little while. Cindy was in good hands with his dad, Bruce, and I hadn't heard any updates otherwise, but I decided not to bring it up that night. Looking straight in his eyes, I was direct as could be. "I've been thinking about you today. I love you, Jett, and I want to be with you, for you. For real."

"For real?" He smiled, squeezing both of my hands in his.

"Yes. I'm sorry that before, I treated you like you were just a part of the plan. I didn't realize how disassociated I've been in life. Living through this plan that I felt was implanted in my brain when I was a child, losing such a large part of my foundation. But I'm here, Jett. I want this more than I want anything else. I mean it." He took a long exhale and contemplated my words. I could tell he was tapping his foot under the table; something he always did before a big exam or a deadline for a paper. *When he was stressed.* As Georgianna plopped down two beautiful floral plates with a giant, gooey roll on each, I watched his mannerisms and wondered if he was even mentally there that moment.

Everything in my body told me not to. *Do not do it, Hailey. You have an image to uphold; you are a young, prudent, Christian woman, and you don't want rumors spread about you, nor do you want to be inappropriate.* That was a family place, after all. But I couldn't help myself. I stood up, leaned over the table, stuck my lips in a perfect pout and closed my eyes. It was up to Jett to reciprocate. While my eyes were closed, I felt the diner go unnaturally quiet. A pair of boots shuffled in my direction, and Jett's lips had still not kissed mine. Instead, someone announced their presence. I peeked my left eye open and saw the silhouette of Colt Wilder standing next to our table,

Jett's cheeks a bright red as they waited for me to shimmy back down in my seat.

"Colt, this is Jett. Jett, this is my coworker, Colt." I held my head in my hands during the entire exchange, because if I didn't look up, it might all have been a dream. Or a vivid nightmare.

"Nice to meet you, man." Colt was the only one to speak as Jett just nodded like he was mute. I didn't blame him, that whole thing was weird how it went down, but I hoped Jett would eventually say *something.* Instead, Colt took the reins.

"So, what do you do, Jett?" Is Colt grilling my boyfriend? Or my soon to be back-on-again boyfriend?

"I just graduated, and I'll be heading to law school next." Colt let out a "huh" noise.

"A lawyer, huh?" He looked over at me, giving me a sharp look in my eyes that I didn't know what it meant. "Well, you two kids have fun on your date." He smiled the way that absolutely irked every nerve in my body, and I had the sudden urge to throw a snowball or bop him over the head with a roll of wrapping paper, but I had nothing handy that wouldn't actually hurt him.

"Thanks. And have fun on your date." He shook his head.

"That's my little sister, Angie. Tomorrow she's heading on a mission trip to Guatemala, so this is her sendoff." My heart softened at the news. While Colt had hinted he was a believer before, it was nice knowing he came from such a solid family with a heart for ministry. I turned my focus back to Jett, who seemed a little down again.

"How are you doing, Jett? With everything." He took a few bites of his cinnamon roll while talking to me about his feelings. He shared that he felt fear for the future and what it would look like without his mother in it.

"I feel completely immobilized. And a mix of guilt, too. On one hand, I know that she's not responding to treatments and receiving palliative care. Our days together are coming to an end. But it feels amazing to be out of the house right now and for that I feel terrible." Listening to him explain his feelings was therapeutic for me, as I too, had unresolved grief for losing my mother. "And I don't want you to think I don't want to be with you, Hailey. I would love to be with you. And seeing you tonight, holding hands, hugging—it feels good. I can't deny that. But—," my heart dropped with that interjection.

"You can't." I said the words for him, my words stoic and without emotion.

"I can't. Not right now. I don't want to drag you along, Hailey. Things might be different in a few months, or weeks. . ." His voice trailed off.

"We don't have to think about the future right now. I'm okay with just this." I took a sip of my hot chocolate and hid my feelings behind the mug. As I started to realize, being in that middle of nowhere town, watching my former boyfriend live through some of the hardest days of his life, my own loneliness was reaching its peak. I didn't want to put that on Jett, as no man could fill my heart, only Jesus—nor take away from what Jett was dealing with—but I knew I needed something to change in my heart in order to be a better woman. I just didn't know what.

CHAPTER 7:
ZERO PERCENT CHANCE OF CHILL

When we arrived at Duckweed Pond, Colt was right: It was stunning. A high mountain lake setting, surrounded by bountiful trees, picnic areas, and lush fragrant bushes. There were a handful of people paddle boarding and a couple in a canoe. All that was missing were the ducks.

Proudly donning an outdoor appropriate set of footwear, a pair of closed toe waterproof shoes , I comfortably walked around in the tall grass. I caught my reflection in the shine of Colt's truck and adjusted the bright yellow silk scarf around my neck. With my rose pink, three-quarter sleeve blazer and white, silk top underneath, I thought I looked ready for a segment about ducks. Holding the baguette I had brought just in case the ducks arrived, I realized all that was missing from my outfit was a beret.

"Do you smell that?" Colt inhaled the air dramatically, releasing his breath with an "ahh" noise.

"Oh no. Did you step in something back there?"

"Very funny, Hailey. No, I'm talking about the beautiful fragrant smell of sagebrush." He plucked a few leaves from a silvery green bush that was bountiful around us and held it to my nose.

"Let me guess, is this a moment where I'm supposed to trust you?" I caught the slightest whiff of its fragrance, and it *was* lovely, but I'd been alive long enough to be weary of smelling anything a man had in his hands.

"Are you always this big of a pain in the rear?" He tossed the leaves over his shoulder and went to his truck. I supposed I had really been busting his chops, but there was just something undeniably annoying about him. Right down to his drop-dead, gorgeous cowboy looks. He was back to wearing the cowboy hat again, which I was pleased about. He must've just not been wearing it that night when I met him at Georgianna's.

"I feel it's my duty to be, otherwise you might start thinking the world revolves around that smile of yours." I looked over and saw him barreling towards me with his heavy camera equipment over his shoulder.

"You saying you like my smile?" He held out his face, beaming ear to ear, just inches from my face as he motioned to his teeth like he was doing a showcase on an infomercial.

"It means I've developed a tolerance to it. Just like my daily caffeine ritual. Or the neighbors' roosters who crow at dawn."

"Ah, caffeine. The best part of everyone's morning. I've certainly seen how much you drink of the stuff." It wasn't a good time to be holding a XXL cup of the stuff at that very moment.

"You know, I'm thinking of switching to tea."

"Mhmm. Sure." We locked eyes for a moment, the tension growing between us. I really wanted to take a sip of my coffee, but I used my remaining strength to set it down on a nearby picnic table.

"Let's get the camera rolling, shall we? I'm ready to get on with my day, Colt." I pulled out my notes that I'd compiled from my chats about the pond with Colt and a quick conversation while I was getting my morning cup of Arabica at Carolina's. It appeared the consensus was, at least on a non-scientific level, the ducks seemed to disappear before weather hit. And they had been gone for an unusual amount of time that month, especially when that time of year brought more in.

"I'm almost ready. . .Just one more. . .Okay, we are rolling in three, two, one. . ." He held up a signal that we were recording.

"This is Hailey Sinclair reporting from the Duckweed Pond, off the Bridge Mountain Pass." I gave a long pause, and he stopped recording. "What did you think of that opening?"

"It was okay." His indifference gave little to interpret.

"Fine. Keep rolling." He motioned again with his countdown, but not a moment after, he stood up tall with eyes wide behind the camera and pointed behind me. As I turned, prepared for anything from a flying car to a grizzly bear, I was relieved to see it was just a goose.

"It's a pond, Colt. I told you; this story is silly. It hasn't been studied closely enough to determine if it's fact or fiction." I held the microphone back up to my face, ready to roll with it regardless if it was a good idea or not. My boss wanted me to do it, so there I was—working for that paycheck.

"I'm not sure, Hailey. That goose is swimming right towards us, working its feet like little paddles. Personally, geese have always been crazy to me. They are territorial on a whole 'nother level; you know what I mean?"

"Sorry, I don't spend a lot of time hanging around waterfowl."

"If I were you, Hailey, I'd put that baguette away. That goose can probably smell it for all I know."

"Do geese even *like* bread? I'm pretty sure that's just a duck thing." I stood my ground, purely because I didn't want to walk back to the truck and put it in there, resetting the whole shot and so on.

"I guess we are about to find out. Rolling in three. . . two. . ." He gave me a thumbs up, and I started talking about the legends of the local waterfowl, being better at predicting weather than most meteorologists. When I finished up my short spiel, I turned and gestured to the pond behind me, while I stood in the beautiful floral gazebo. Fat roses of yellow, pink and white were woven into a bright green ivy that was wrapped around all the beams. It really was romantic there. Speaking again about the beauty and calmness of the lake, I was distracted by Colt's laughter.

"What is it now?" I put my microphone to my side in a huff.

"I told you, Hailey. He smells the bread!" Just then the squawk of a large, white winged creature flew right into the gazebo, knocking me down on my side as I screamed in fright. His wings were flapping loud and fast, but I was able to toss the baguette to the other side of the gazebo.

"Do something, Colt! This bird is not right in the head!" I screamed through the chaos, but Colt was either fresh out of ideas or cares, because he was laughing his rear end off outside of the gazebo.

A voice was heard from the distance. "Do *not* show fear! They smell fear."

"Thanks!" I yelled back, feeling *so* much better knowing I already had viewership while it was happening live. The goose seemed not to care about the baguette, which at least gave me a win. *Right?*

Colt keeled over from laughter as I calmed down, seeing the goose wasn't attacking me, nor had it. My eyes were still intact, and with them I saw the goose was waltzing around me like it was sizing me up for a game of dodgeball. "He wants something from me. Help me, please!" I rolled to my stomach, getting up on my feet in a jump position, and the goose started acting up again. Colt finally jumped into action and ran towards the goose, hoping to scare it off. It worked. Breathlessly, I gave him a piece of my mind.

"Are all of your story ideas going to be animal related? Newsflash, Colt: I am a meteorologist, not a zookeeper!"

"I promise you, that wasn't planned. But was it amazing? A resounding yes."

It happened quickly after that. The swooping wing from the bird's flaps came back faster, taking a nosedive approach right for my neck. Colt jumped in front of the bird, as I stumbled, falling out of the gazebo and into the soft grass. The goose went around Colt, who was now flapping his arms and yelling, as if he was fighting the goose with the logic of a grizzly bear, and the unhinged waterfowl went straight for my neck, plucking the end of the scarf and taking the whole bright yellow silk piece of fabric with it. Colt, not missing a beat, grabbed me by the backs of my arms and lifted me up in one fell swoop. He stayed there, our faces *too* close together for a split second as I steadied in his grasp. With his hands holding me up, I felt fireworks run through my veins.

He was close. Close enough that I could smell his spearmint gum that he'd been chewing incessantly on the drive in. But as I looked at him, my heart began to soften. I found the secrets to the universe in the gold specs of his eyes. The way the corners of his mouth turned up ever so slightly when he looked at me made my heart skip a beat. The strong, masculine features of his prominent nose and jawline reflected the unshakable steadiness in his character.

At that moment, I caught my breath and rebuked the thoughts. No, this wasn't the time, or the man. Just because Jett had left my heart aching, didn't mean it needed to be wandering. As I thought that, Colt took a step back and returned to his camera. *Lord, please keep my eyes where they belong, my thoughts pure, and my heart even more so.*

I scanned the water and skies for the goose, but he was long gone. For that, I was thankful. "Darn." Colt shot his eyes back to me, as I started wiping off the grass from my black pants, thankful nothing happened to my blazer or white blouse. "I guess that goose really needed a pop of color." He chuckled, and I prayed that our near-miss, or rather, near-*kiss* was behind us now.

"I'm a little disappointed the ducks aren't back. There's nothing cuter than the little ducklings."

"I have a feeling if we stay long enough, that goose might have some goslings it wants to protect. Maybe I could be the one behind the camera this time? We could submit the tape as a tryout for you to be on Animal Planet."

"That's the first good idea you've had all day, Hailey. You'll find I have a real way with animals, especially poultry birds. I'm a real chick magnet, if you catch my drift."

"More like, tick magnet." I pointed to a bug crawling on his forearm.

"Touche." He flicked it off.

The drive back to the station was quieter than it had been previously, since I wasn't trying to drown out his words with the radio. I found myself feeling uncomfortable in his silence and decided to pepper him with a few questions.

"How was the rest of your night? With your sister, Angie."

"Really nice, thanks for asking. I love that kid. She's going to do great things in the world."

"Is, uh, she the one who had the crush on Jett?" My curiosity got the best of me.

"No, that's my other sister, Mandy. She's about to turn 21. Her and Jett went to high school together; he was just a year older is all." I felt a little bit of jealousy in my gut as I learned that they were close to the same age. But since Jett told me he hadn't dated in high school, I wasn't too worried about it. Colt continued. "She actually almost told him her feelings for him the night before he left for college. Had it all worked out that she was going to knock on his parents front door and spill her heart. She came down with chickenpox and never got the chance." Colt started laughing. "I encouraged her to go tell him anyway, full body rash or not. She refused. We still call her '*chicken*' to this day." Wow, it sounded like more than a crush, but full-blown feelings. Huh. "Then he comes home from college and rumor has it, he's got a girlfriend." Colt pointed to me, but his finger was like a dagger.

"That must have really hurt Mandy. I'm sorry."

"Aww. Don't be sorry; be happy you got your man. You've won the prize of Jett Dawson." He put his hand through the air like he was revealing a rainbow.

I smiled, trying my best not to shrug, and thankfully stoicism was my superpower. I could show zero emotion when I needed to most, like right then. Colt did not need to know that Jett couldn't decide if he wanted to be with me or join the monks, and I was thankful he didn't.

"So, what's next for us?" Colt asked, looking straight out onto the road.

"Excuse me?" I knew we had some *serious* chemistry back there, but I thought it was unspoken that we didn't bring it up again. Like, ever.

"There's an alpaca farm out on Route 14. I'm thinking we should go out after a rainstorm, put some animal feed in our back pockets. I bet you we could find ourselves in a little trouble. Some real Emmy's gold."

Back at the station, I saw in two days' time, we'd be getting a solid rainstorm with some hail. Hopefully, the ducks would return after that.

*****

The next several weeks were filled with windy weather reports and every kind of segment you could think of from the hailstorm that destroyed an entire fleet of used trucks at the car dealership, to the rapid snowmelt run-off causing flash flooding into ditches. An entire home's foundation was wiped out, yet the home remained intact. Colt was right; Wyoming had some crazy weather.

The ducks did return to the Duckweed Pond, and our segment caught the eye of an out-of-state waterfowl expert who shared our clip to reach greater heights. Our viewership was through the roof, and Nick was hiring more staff. He gave Colt and I complete creative freedom to do reporting on what we felt was relevant, but to Colt's credit, he came up with all of the stories. We were spending a lot of time together, and while it seemed there was always running, dodging, or screaming happening when we were filming, I made sure to not put myself in a position where we'd be locked in like that again.

Jett had completely pulled away from me, however. Though we were not officially together, outside of us and his parents, no one knew that. I actually appreciated how much pressure it took off of me in that department because when you have the label of being single, every married person in a 500-

mile vicinity—whether they are happy or not—has it out to change that on your behalf. And truthfully, I didn't know if I could handle Colt knowing. Since Jett and I had broken up right after I got there, and I still cared for him and hoped he'd come around, I never bothered to tell anyone otherwise. It simply wasn't their business, and besides, it wasn't the fate I wanted. But all of that was about to change, and I wished I'd been given a heads up.

One day, after a long-winded report at the town's county fair, Colt and I had been investigating reports that the carousel had been struck by lightning and afterward, it ran without power. We were highly suspicious of the story, but since we were already there, we decided to see the thing in action. The man running the carousel was holding up the cord —proving it was plugged into nothing—as it spun around; albeit, it was moving too fast to be safe, and thankfully, it wasn't allowing passengers. We joked about our taglines for the story— "*The Carousel That Could.*'" The station's ViralVideo channel was starting to generate revenue, and Nick was learning about the power of clickbait, so we were always teasing funny captions or titles for the videos. After filming a brief clip of the carousel, we decided to walk around for a few minutes.

"Want me to win you a bear?" Colt pointed to the wall of colorful stuffed plushies.

"I'd love to see you try. These games are rigged," I snickered, secretly enjoying that he asked. He waltzed over to a shooting game, a little *too* confident, and said, "Watch this." With that ego, I knew I was in for something good. But when he hit every single bottle he aimed for, I didn't realize a talent for carnival games was something I'd ever be impressed by.

"Not you again, Colt." The woman working the game walked over. "I knew I recognized you. I thought I'd run you off for good last time you were here with your sisters." She reached out with open arms and gave him a hug.

"Nice to see you, Layla. I'm afraid I can't stay away." She gave Colt the choice of stuffed bears, and he picked a pink one with a heart on its tummy. "See you next year," he called over his shoulder, to which she nodded. We walked over to a table, and he handed me the bear. "As promised." I took it, knowing full well this was the only one with a heart on it, so while half of me felt annoyed as ever at how cute it was, the other half of my brain wanted to return it to him. Instead, I sat it on the table and didn't acknowledge it.

"Thanks. Come here a lot?"

"Yeah. My uncle used to have a few of these carnival games in his house. Whenever I'd go over there, which was often, I'd master them. Worked out really well when I brought dates here in my teens."

"I can't tell if you're implying a high frequency of that event or you only had dates during the carnival, since it's here but three days a year. Maybe they were just using you for the stuffed bears." My phone started buzzing in my pocket. It was Jett. "Hold that thought. I'm dying to know more about these carny dates." I stood up and walked a few feet away so I could have a private conversation, as Jett did not call me often. He simply would send a text.

"It's time, Hailey." My heart sank as I answered the phone.

"Time for what?"

"Hospice." Tears welled in my eyes. I had popped in on Cindy every few days, but I didn't see her struggles. She had been staying so strong for her family, friends and me. While I knew the day would come, I never expected it to be so soon.

"Can I come?" Instantly choked up, I couldn't hold it back any longer.

"Yes. Can you come now? They are administering morphine already. She's off her meds. The focus now is keeping her comfortable."

"I'm about thirty minutes from Big Horn, so I'll be there in forty-five."

"Okay."

"I'm sorry, Jett."

"Me, too." We ended the call. Colt took one look at my face and knew something was very wrong.

"Jett's mom. I gotta go." He agreed, sending me off with words of encouragement.

"I'll be here praying."

CHAPTER 8:

THE CHAOS BEFORE THE STORM

The carpet felt soft on my bare feet. I had been wearing muck boots constantly those days, and it felt good to kick them off when I arrived at Jett's parents' house. I didn't even have to knock before he opened the door with his bloodshot eyes. The house was quiet as a church mouse.

"Is she here?" I whispered, not wanting to disturb anything. He nodded.

"She's in her room. And she's excited to see you." I gave Jett a hug, holding him deeper than I ever have. I waited for him to let go, and when he didn't, I gave him a soft, friendly peck on the cheek and released his embrace. "It's nice to see you. I'm glad you came."

"Of course. Thank you for letting me know." I tiptoed down the small hallway of their immaculate home. When I reached her door, it was open, and she was smiling at me. Bruce was in the corner of the room, tidying up.

"There's my girl. Come have a seat right here." Her bed had been moved to the side of the room and in its place was a large hospital bed. She was sitting up in it, as it moved with a remote at her left side. "Look at this fancy bed. Pretty cool, right?" Always in good spirits, I marveled at the pure joy she encapsulated. I sat down, and though I tried my absolute hardest not to, I broke out in a hard, ugly cry. I heard Bruce leave and the door closed behind him.

"I—I'm so sorry, Cindy. You just don't deserve this," I choked out the words.

"But I do, my dear. I get to meet Jesus early. And be in His glory." Her mannerisms looked frail as she took me by the hand. "Listen, Hailey. You're a good girl, with a heart for Jesus. And I know you love my son." I looked up at her and wiped away my tears with my free hand. "I love you like a daughter, and I see your struggles." She paused. "Love is a gift. Everyone we get to love is a blessing from the Lord. But sometimes, He has people go their separate ways in order to grow. And it's okay to let go of our past. Because the future—His plans? They are so much greater, Hailey." The tears flowed. I wasn't ready to say goodbye to Cindy, or Jett.

"You want me to walk away from him? But I love him."

"I want you to do what God is calling you to do, Hailey. I know you love him. So do I. He's a wonderful man. But is he the right man for you?" I felt like a weight was being lifted off of me but instantly replaced with guilt for feeling that way.

"I know I've battled with loneliness and fear. But turning my back on him now—even the hope of us getting back together, that I know isn't real—feels worse than anything."

"Just pray about it, Hailey. Maybe you two get married and have six children and three cats. Maybe you don't. But I just want to give you permission that it's okay to let go. Following God's plan requires bravery and guts." She squeezed my hand gently.

"Thank you, Cindy." We sat in silence for a few minutes as I contemplated her words. When she asked me about work, I told her about the day's stories we filmed at the county fair. We both had a good laugh at the antics.

"This Colt is a real character." She smiled, knowingly, and a few more tears came.

"I just can't say goodbye, Cindy. I've been running from this since my own mother passed, cut myself off from all love, and finally I have comfort in your family, but I'm losing every piece of it." Cindy looked at me lovingly.

"But my dear, you are gaining the comfort of Christ. He is near to the brokenhearted. I just know you will be okay. I promise." Giving her hand a squeeze, I said what I knew would be my final goodbye.

"I'll keep sending you those funny memes you like, and I'll come by whenever you want. I'll even bring a movie." The rest of Cindy's time was for her family but making promises like those helped cushion the hurt.

"I hope you do. We watch you on the news every weeknight. I keep holding out hope for one last good storm, like we had here when I was a kid. The power would go out; the shutters would rattle. Lightning bolts right in the front yard!"

"While I can't make any promises about that, I'll send a prayer to the man upstairs." I kissed her forehead, leaving behind a piece of my heart.

I stopped in the hallway bathroom before facing Jett and wiped my eyes and face with a wet washcloth. No use making it any more real for him than it had to be. He was waiting in the living room when I came out.

"Thank you for coming." Jett stood, as he spoke platonically, like we were old friends. And I faced the music, for the second time in an hour: I didn't have the feelings for him I thought I did. I had lingered out of guilt and fear of being lonely.

Jett was comfortable, and if Cindy hadn't pointed that out, I may have spent the rest of my life loitering around the idea.

"Thank you, Jett. For sharing your wonderful life and family with me. For giving me companionship over these last few years that would have been much harder without you. And for leading me here to Wyoming. It's crazy to say, but it's not so bad of a place." Jett nodded, smiling. "I'm sorry, I know this isn't the time to talk about me." I gave him a hug and went to the door.

"Hailey," Jett spoke, softly. I turned, facing him again. "Thank you for seeing something in me. I might not have been ready for all of that but having you by my side during this time has been the honor of a lifetime."

As I sat in my car after leaving, I prayed to God for comfort for the family, myself, and a path to follow.

*****

I went home before returning to the station, showered, and did one of those freezer eye masks that make you look like a bandit and make your forehead feel like you've eaten ice cream too fast, but depuff your eyes in seconds. After some reflection, I did find peace and comfort in the situation at hand.

I was able to return to work an hour later to do my analysis and studying, before giving a sparkling weather report.

As I pulled up all my softwares, a big anomaly caught my eye. Something that wasn't there yesterday. Heck, something that wasn't there when I first looked at it that morning.

Pulling up the historical averages for the last several decades, it appeared that the area got around twelve inches of rain on average per year. It was considered the high desert, so that didn't surprise me. What did surprise me, and was creating some serious confusion, was that there was a supercell storm coming over the area a few days from that day which was going to somehow be isolated over Big Horn, Wyoming. It would be gaining strength from our side of the mountains and dumping several inches—if not feet—of moisture on us like we were a bullseye. High winds would be hurricane speeds. "This can't be right," I said aloud, pouring over the data. I took a few computer screenshots and opened an email for my college professor to check it. *I must be missing something, right?* I hashed out a quick email and spent another hour poring over it again and again.

As Colt said, the weather there changed fast. I learned that fast, within my first week noticing that on a five- day forecast, it could substantially change three days later. The night lows would rise, and the daytime highs would lower substantially, then vice versa. I often wondered how anyone in the weather forecasting industry kept any accountability there with things being so. . . complicated. A knock on the door caught me off guard. Speaking of complicated, it was Colt.

"Hey, you doing alright?" Colt looked annoyingly more handsome than usual that afternoon, and I couldn't put my finger on it.

"Yes, thank you for asking." I didn't want to bring it up or even think about it, given that I'd be going on air in under an hour.

"So, I was thinking; the baseball field was destroyed in that wind storm last weekend. All the bases blew away, and the dirt even ran over the painted lines."

"Let me guess; there's a mountain lion that guards it at night, and you're hoping for a good on-air chase? Count me out." My words came out harsher than I intended, but he smiled anyway, always giving me a little grace when I needed it most.

"Nah, nothing like that. I was thinking we could do a little segment on it to raise funds. I can't imagine all the little leaguers out there with no place to play." *Lord, please soften my heart. I did not expect that.*

"That's a lovely idea. Sure, I'm in."

Colt grinned. "You also, uh, forgot this today." He sat the plump, pink stuffed bear with a heart on its tummy next to my computer.

How much had changed since earlier that day. I was excited to have it. "That was kind of you, Colt. Thank you." I meant my words.

"I think that's the nicest thing you've ever said to me." He clutched his heart, dramatically.

"Don't make me regret it. Now get." I swatted him out, and he backed away, laughing, but not before throwing one more shot my way.

"I do know of a good fishing hole that the bears like to frequent—,"

I cut him off, deciding then that the weather system was very much real and would be happening *soon*. "Not if it was the last story on earth, Colt. I'm going to have to pass on that." His smile turned to mischief. My mind went back to the storm. If it was legitimate, I had better have announced it immediately. Things like that were not to be held back. "I have news. Looks like there's a historic weather system coming. I don't have all the details yet, as things are changing quickly, but I have a feeling we are going to have plenty to report on in the coming weeks."

"Really? Tell me about that, Hailey. My brother's got a head of one-hundred-and-fifty cattle and about a third of those are calves. That's some pretty important information to keep to yourself." He almost seemed mad, and I clicked back to check my emails, hitting the refresh button. While they loaded, as the internet was pretty glacially paced out there, I rattled off what I knew.

"Nothing is for sure yet. This is so out of left field according to the data that I have, which goes back over a hundred years. I've consulted my college professor to be safe, and as a matter of fact, here's an email from her right now." I opened it up, reading it aloud. "*Dear Hailey, Thank you for your message. I am very excited to hear that you have secured a position as a meteorologist at a news station in Wyoming. While I had to re-familiarize myself with where that is on a map, it sounds nonetheless like an adventure.*

"*Looking at the data you sent, you are right; that is quite alarming. You have it correct that if the storm stays in the path that it is, you will be hit with a historic amount of rainfall over a 24-hour period. Hope you are building an ark. Just kidding, but please be safe. Call me anytime. I'm leaving my number below.*

Prof. Sarah Lehman"

Colt's jaw dropped so low, I thought it might hit the floor. "And when does this start, Hailey?"

"Six days from today. I just wanted to consult her to be sure, as nothing on this scale has ever happened here on record."

"You're right about that. We better let the people know so they can prepare."

Colt and I jumped into action immediately, preparing a pre-recorded message that would play at the start of the news, in addition to my scheduled live report. He also alerted the newspaper, the hospital, and all emergency services, including the Red Cross. For a moment, we sat in silence, waiting for both the literal and figurative storm to come, in response to our alerts.

A few calls started rolling in, and I did my best to field questions. I told them to pass on the answers to their friends and neighbors, which they said they would do. Nick, who was at first in disbelief, offered a really good suggestion.

"Perhaps the lobby of the station could be a staging ground for emergency supplies. Water, blankets, candles. Things like that."

Colt responded, "If the storm hits as hard as we think it is, the station is going to need sandbags and waterproofing. Our front doors don't stand a chance against the power of water. But I love that idea, Nick. How about we instead move it to the Grace Point Church? It's the largest in town, and they've got those giant storm doors leading into an entryway with stairs going up. It would be a great base camp for people in need of both shelter and supplies."

While Nick and Colt plotted it out, I said a prayer for the safety of the community that I was not only welcomed into with open arms, but starting to love. I returned to my office to check the weather for the millionth time that day. For what it seemed, Cindy was getting her storm.

Colt and I went out to the edge of the reservoir to shoot a video about the upcoming storm. He would add our radar videos to the footage, and for the first time, I felt like I was doing some real meteorology. As I spoke on camera, a large gusty cross wind blew my hair to the other side of my head. I continued on, used to it by that point. Colt smiled.

A moment later, I started up again. "As you can see behind me, the water levels here at Togwotee Reservoir are already high due to this year's snow melt. Any rise in the levels here will be significant, and. . ." I stepped backwards, trying to move, so Colt could have a clearer shot of what I was referring to when my foot stepped into some sort of mud hole, but Colt did not take the camera off of me for a second. I smiled, looking up at the camera, and in my most professional voice, continued, ". . .and, it appears that I am now one with the earth. You see, these are the sort of problems that recreators can be warned about when we have too much moisture in the ground." Colt zoomed out, getting my full body in the picture. "The ground can become a quicksand of sorts, due to the high moisture content, soil composition, and lack of structure. It appears I will need a tow rope to get out of this. You've been warned." I smiled blankly, waiting for Colt to cut the feed before I could freak out. I thought I could feel all sorts of creepy crawlies on my foot, that thankfully, had been in a nice dry muck boot. But since it only came to my ankle, which was rapidly disappearing, I was growing more anxious by the moment.

"A little help here?"

"Alright, alright. Give me a second. You're not going to sink." As he spoke the words, I dropped a few more inches.

"Are you sure about that?"

He walked over to me at an annoyingly normal pace, put his hands in my underarms and lifted me out like I was weightless, setting me back on dry ground.

I straightened my hair, tossing it back to a center part, and thanked him. He was smiling the rest of the time we were together.

Our storm was the main topic of the nightly news every day of the week leading up to it. Community members had been coming out of the woodwork to prepare, and the stores were wiped out of bread and milk within the first day. Thankfully, extra trucks of supplies were sent and delivered to the grocery stores and Grace Point Church, who agreed to be the base camp for safety for the community.

Every farmer in the county was slammed moving animals to higher ground to which I was just waiting for Colt to get called away for. Three days before the storm hit, I came into the station first thing, already hearing the wind howling down the canyon. I was there more than I wasn't those last few days, and thankfully, Carolina had been bringing large pots of coffee over for the whole crew, so instead of going to The Rusted Mug, I'd been seeing her there. She was just arriving when I was still standing in the lobby that morning, greeting Nancy. I ran to open the door for her, as her hands were full.

"Good morning, Carolina."

She beamed a beautiful smile. "Good morning to you ladies. I made several batches of chocolate scones and pumpkin cookies. All this weather talk, and I can't help but nest."

As she set down the large box filled with treats and two coffee pots on the table, Nancy and I were drawn to the contents like a magnet.

Immediately filling my tumbler with fresh Arabica, something out of the corner of my eye caught my attention. I nearly jumped for joy. "Are you sure it's the weather? Or is it that?" I pointed to the beautiful, purple gemstone ring on her finger that perfectly fit her spunky style.

"Oh, this old thing? Yeah, it might be the fact that I'm getting married." She stretched her arm all the way out while Nancy and I congratulated and hugged her.

"I just knew that Nick was going to find some bravery and ask you to marry him. After all these years of him pining away for you, I assumed he'd propose before even the first date," Nancy giggled away while she took a bite of the dreamy pumpkin cookies with candied pecans and a marshmallow filling.

I was already on my second cookie. "When is the big day, have you set a date yet?" I asked.

"It's going to be soon, just a few months away, actually. Nick wants to do it September 4th, because that was the first day he saw me, though it was in the third grade." Carolina blushed, and we fawned over how cute their love story was.

It was the epitome of patience and letting things flow naturally rather than trying to control them, which I was never good at. I could learn so much from those around me.

"There she is." Nick came eagerly to the lobby and embraced Carolina in a modest hug and small kiss. "How's the most beautiful woman in the world doing today? Do I smell treats?" He spoke to her gently and in observing their interaction, while he carefully selected a few baked goods and looked at them in marvel before savoring each bite, he treated her like she was the rarest gem in the world. It was beautiful, and I prayed to God that one day I would have a relationship built in love and respect like this, rather than fear of being alone, like I had with Jett.

I shuffled away to my office, taking the last of my cookie with me. A knock on the door came instantaneously.

"Hailey," Colt said, walking in and putting his phone in his pocket.

"Yes, Colt?" I wondered why he was addressing me so formally.

"I've got to go for a few days. Need to help my brother move the cattle to high ground. I promise I will be back by the time the storm hits, okay? Just be safe. Please."

I didn't want to admit it, but I was unexpectedly sad that he was leaving. "Oh great, what about the video we were going to make of me, in the eye of the storm, swinging from a tree?" I snickered at him, annoyed more at my feelings than anything.

"I would never put you in danger, Hailey."

"Yeah, right. May I remind you of Filbert? Or better yet, the deranged goose who is a scarf thief? I had that thing for years just waiting for the perfect opportunity to wear it, and now I'll never get a chance again." Colt snickered and looked down at his feet. "That's fine, though. I get it. The animals need our help in this world. Go be the cowboy that Big Horn needs." I smiled at him, hoping to come off encouraging rather than sarcastic, but as always with Colt, I had trouble with that.

"You're not. . .mad?"

I was taken back by his question. "Why would I be mad? The animals need you. I don't." It was rude, and I regretted the words, but as always, Colt gave me grace.

"You're impossible, you know that?" He smiled at me, not taking his eyes off of me.

"And yet, here you are." I leaned back in my chair, crossing my arms.

"Listen. . .If I'm not back before things get rough, just promise me you'll stay safe. Go to Grace Point Church and weather it there if you have to. Don't try to be brave. Or reckless."

"I'm a meteorologist, Colt. I know what the weather can do, and I promise, I'm not going to be out trying to fly a kite in it."

"I just don't want anything to happen to you." His words were soft but still gave off an incredibly annoying big-brother energy.

"What's next, a permission slip to drive home? Relax, Wilder. I'll be fine." I gave him a side eye glare, fighting my lips as hard as I could not to smile. It was rather cute to see him worried, I thought. Returning to my computer, I started typing away to avoid more conversation. When he finally turned to leave, I watched him walk down the hallway in his full cowboy getup. If he promised to be back by the time it hit, then that storm couldn't come soon enough.

CHAPTER 9:

IN THE EYE OF THE STORM

I was disappointed to see Ben, our fill-in cameraman, standing at Colt's post as we filmed a few storm tips that afternoon. It was Nick's idea, and I enjoyed doing it. If Colt were there, we would've skipped the green screen and went to find some crazy backdrop of dust blowing around instead, so I appreciated that I got to stay warm and dry inside at least. I was just wrapping up a part about downed power poles when Nick scattered away. Ben cut the tape, and while I reviewed my notes for what was next, Nick came sauntering back in, soaking wet.

"What happened to you, man?" Ben hollered at Nick's alarming appearance. He had just been dry a moment ago, and his tan dress shirt soaked to his body let us know he'd been hiding some pretty nice muscles under his ill-fitted suits. I found myself looking at him a little differently. Maybe a tad more respect than I already had.

"I just thought I heard something outside, so I went out to check," Nick was almost breathless, "and the rain just picked up."

"Man, that isn't the rain that I know. You look like you tripped and fell into a pool at a baby shower while avoiding your in-laws." We both looked at Ben.

"Speaking from experience?" I asked.

"Something like that," Ben nodded.

"There is nothing on the radar, anywhere, Nick. I've been looking at it all day." I walked to the front doors and looked outside. Sure enough, it was torrential. I picked up the pace and went to my office, rapidly clicking on browsers to open the weather portal back up. As I clicked the buttons to refresh, my window outside reflected a bright patch of blue skies opening up and as quickly as it started, the rain ended.

"What in the world was that?" The radar showed a small, fast moving storm cell that popped up out of nowhere, wrung itself out like a towel above us, and then dissipated.

"Never mind, Hailey," Nick hollered from down the hall.

I got up to talk to him.

"It's over, now. But I'm telling you, if that was even a fraction of what's coming, this town is in no way shape or form prepared."

Nick shook out his hair like a wet dog while I stood in the doorway of my office, avoiding the spray. If only Colt was here, he would have some annoying solution like always to make sure we were extra prepared.

Nick reached into his pocket and pulled out his phone. "No way!"

"What?" I took a gulp of my coffee, knowing I needed more to prepare for whatever fresh issue that could be.

"Hailey, you've gone *viral.*"

"Huh? Like, *Big Horn, Wyoming* viral, or *viral* viral?" He held up his phone. My latest video where Colt and I went to the edge of the town's reservoir, and I got stuck in the mud hole, went viral. For real. Worldwide, by the looks of the numbers. Watching it again, I couldn't grasp why that video, of all of our hits, was the one to be so popular. "Wow. I'm shocked." The views kept going upward, well into the millions by then.

"Woohoo! We've done it guys! Hailey, expect a bonus in your check when we start getting monetization from these videos."

That was good news, as while my salary wasn't horrendous, it certainly left little room to dream of a life outside of Big Horn. "I just can't help but wonder, why out of all of our videos, it's this one? I've been chased by a menace goat wearing a *sweater*, Nick."

Nick laughed as he recalled the video.

"Umm.. My mistake, Hailey. All of the videos are going viral." He handed me his phone which was the homepage for the station's ViralVideo account, and it was true; our subscribers had gone up hundreds of thousands in just a day.

"I'm speechless." We had two more days till the storm hit, and while we all wanted to celebrate our online win, we quickly got back to work preparing for what was to come.

*****

The next day, I stayed home a little while in the morning, putting rolled up towels against doors and making sure all of my windows were completely sealed. A knock on the door made my heart drop. Who could that be? I peeked out the window next to the door to see it was a delivery driver, plopping a large brown box off by my door. Grabbing the package and hollering thanks to the driver, I tore the box open with a bread knife from the kitchen.

Inside was a beautiful pair of rain navy boots, with a delicate, bright pink floral pattern, complete with a matching coat and umbrella. I pulled out the coat, that was solid navy without the pattern. It was a beautiful, classy set. At the bottom of the box, I pulled out a note. They were a gift from my father.

So proud of you and all of your accomplishments, kiddo. You are never far from my thoughts. I know your mother would be proud. I wiped a tear from my eye at the gesture. I had given his wife my address a week ago, before all of the storm tracking started, and I hadn't thought about it since. I was genuinely touched by the gift.

I decided it was the perfect outfit to wear that day, along with some fitted khaki trousers and a coordinating pink sweater. The coat came to my thighs, and it had a little drawstring pull around the middle, so my waist didn't get lost in it. It was certainly the most flattering rain outfit I'd ever seen, and it would look tasteful for my segment on air that night, as Ben and I would be shooting on location at his family's farm that overlooked much of the valley. I texted a photo of me in it, along with a note of thanks to my father.

When I made it to the station, I worked in my office for a while, keeping my phone close by. The storm was projected to hit that night, and knowing how variable things were, I was assuming a 6-hour window for when it could make landfall. If we were on the coast, the winds alone would have been considered a Category 1 hurricane. When I was finished, I checked my phone again, as if I would've missed the dinging notification of a message. Where in the world was Colt? He said he'd be back by then.

"Hey, Hailey." I looked up eagerly, expecting to see Colt. It was Ben. I tried to hide my disappointment.

"Ben. You ready to go?"

"I sure am. Do you want to follow, or ride together? It's easy access."

"I'll follow." I gathered my things and did just that.

The drive to Ben's family farm was scenic, but in the way of dirt roads leading up a mountain. Though my car could handle it, I wanted to have a chat with him on what he meant by "easy access." Colt would have driven me, but then again, Ben did offer, so I couldn't be mad about that. We reached the acreage and set up a beautiful shot of the valley. I looked out to the landscape and took a big gulp of the fresh, mountain air. The lands were so green, it nearly hurt my eyes. You could see small herds of elk in fields to the left, and antelope in some of the higher plains. Fresh snow was in the mountains, despite it being June, but I enjoyed its beauty and thanked God for His wondrous creation.

A dark cluster of storm clouds could be seen a few miles away, scattered at the time, but soon to create a supercell. An uneasy feeling washed over me; I wanted to finish it fast and get to Grace Point Church where I'd promised Colt I'd weather the storm.

Ben took heed at my request to do a quick segment and started rolling the tape. I gave a short analysis, referring to the storm clouds in the distance and asked everyone to stay safe and sound, reminding them about the local services available, and what to do in a power outage. He cut the footage, and I got back in my car, taking the tape with me. Ben was going to stay and ride out the storm with his family, and Nick would edit the tape and put it on air.

Back at the station, Nick put together the whole show ahead of time, using all of our prerecorded footage, heeding Colt's warning about the station being no match for the water. After finishing up the technical parts, we all pitched in and made sure the place was as secure as it could be before leaving. Some went home; some went to Grace Point Church. When I pulled up in the parking lot, the wind was starting to blow like crazy, and raindrops were hitting the car sideways. While they had a covered area for people to park, they were recommending not to, as that structure could collapse under the right circumstances, so I parked in the center of the lot, and was almost instantaneously surrounded by cars. I was trapped.

When I was traversing the lot, my phone buzzed. It was Colt. My heart skipped a beat. "Hi."

"Hailey." He sounded out of breath. Where are you?" I could hear his truck running in the background.

"I've just gotten to Grace Point. And where are you?" My tone was firm.

"I'm still on the road. I should be there in twenty minutes, but the weather even just up the canyon here is already bad. Expect it to hit town anytime."

"Thanks for the update, I'll be sure to tell the others. See you soon." I ended the call, my phone ringing almost immediately again. I answered without even looking. "Don't worry, I'm inside." I said in my usual snarky tone.

"It's Jett." I looked at my phone, pulling it back in disbelief. Yep, it sure was.

"Hi! Are you okay? The storm is about to hit."

"She's got hours left, Hailey. If you want to come. I know this is crazy timing." My heart sank. I did want to go. I wanted to go more than anything in my life, and the fact that I was invited made me feel like if I didn't go, I'd be letting down more than just Cindy. Jett and Bruce, too.

"I'm going to try my best, Jett. I promise."

"Okay. Be careful, Hailey. And thank you." I hung up and ran back outside to my car. It was closed on all sides by several cars in each row. People were still pulling in and parking without abandon just to get into the lot. A loud crack of thunder erupted in the sky, and all the lights in the nearby vicinity went off like someone flipped the switch. We had been warned by the power company that the transformers were weakened already, so there were no promises it would hold. Thankfully, Grace Point had a generator, so its lights gloriously whipped back on without another thought.

"God, what am I going to do?" I called out for help, tears welling in my eyes. I wanted to be with Cindy as she met Jesus, but I had no way of getting there. Just then, a loud truck revved into the lot. Colt.

Waving my arms hysterically as I ran towards him, the little hood on my coat not working fast enough to repel the raindrops as they ramped up, Colt hopped out, his truck still running.

"Are you okay!?" he yelled, running towards me.

"It's Cindy, Jett's mom. She's got hours left, Colt."
Tears running down my face, he grabbed my hand, and we ran
to the truck, wind whipping hard against us. When he opened
the passenger door, I thought it might rip right off if he wasn't
holding on to it, so he did. I almost fell getting into the truck,
but he pushed me up into it with his other free hand. When he
got into the driver's side, he started driving like he stole it, all
the way into the storm. On the way there, the weather raged.
His windshield wipers went erratically. As we crossed a bridge
over part of a river, a tree was struck by lightning next to us,
and I screamed at the scare. Colt picked up the speed.

"This is reckless, Hailey. But I'm doing my best to get
you there."

"If anyone can, it's you, Colt." My tears just wouldn't
stop. It was the first time I had shown emotion around Colt, and
I could tell he was trying to process it as he drove us in silence.

"I don't know about that." A break in the wind enabled
us to get the rest of the way to Jett's place without incident,
but the rain was raging. As he pulled up, he parked sideways so
I could get out dry.

"Stay right here; you don't need to get out. I'll be right
back." I promised him I would only be there a few minutes as it

was dangerous being out, especially in that valley as it ran along the river.

"I think we got fifteen minutes before that dam washes out." He pointed to a low spot on the river behind us. "But it won't hurt any of these houses; it just might take the road up there with it." The road we needed to get back to Grace Point.

"Roger that." I used his line and raced to the front door, not bothering to knock. Jett heard me, and I fumbled with my rain boots trying to get them off.

"Hailey, in here."

My heart was racing a hundred miles an hour as I walked back into the room to see her one last time. Her eyes were closed, but she was still with us, judging by her smile.

"She stopped talking, but I know she can hear us." Bruce, not leaving her side, was holding her left hand while Jett was holding her right. It was a beautiful moment of love and devotion from her family. I was honored to witness it. I prayed to God for help.

"Cindy," I whispered, her smile gently rolling across her face. I suddenly felt the peace of the Holy Spirit wash over me. She knew I was there. Words didn't mean anything right then. She was about to meet Jesus. And not a moment later, she took her last breath, with all of us by her side.

"Are you alright?" Colt asked me as I got back into his truck. I felt stunned. I couldn't care less about how I looked, though I knew it had to be rough.

"I will be. Thank you. Let's go before we can't." Having just said my tearful goodbyes to Jett and Bruce, I wondered what they were going to do . I suppose the only thing they could do was pray.

Colt tore back through the canyon as the rain pelted us from every direction. I looked through his back window; his truck bed was starting to flood. As we went through the winding roads along the river, we were halfway back to town when a loud crack was heard in front of us. Colt slowed the truck, not seeing where it was coming from as we both looked all around, cautiously.

"Look! A tree is coming down!" I yelled, as a tall pine tree fell into the road, blocking it completely from passing.

"Oh no!" Colt hollered, his voice muffled under the rain that was now turning to hail. "This is not a good place to weather the storm. We've got to find shelter and fast." He looked all around for a moment. "I know where we are. Tim Garth has a ranch right over there." Colt pointed to a hillside. I couldn't see anything but the water pouring all over the truck. "Can you climb over to this side? You're on the side of the river, and I can't see if it's flooding."

"Yes, I can." I shimmied over to the driver's side, over his cupholders and gear shifters. He took my hand and opened the truck door, but the wind instantly lashed it shut again. We both looked at each other in fear.

"Hailey, this is going to sound crazy, but we are going to need to use the wind to our favor."

"Okay, let's do it. You've gotten me this far; I'm not going to give up here."

"There's a big, sturdy barn on that hillside. It's got a strong frame with metal beams, built a few years ago. I helped him pour the concrete for it, so I've seen it up close. I trust it. We gotta make a run for it. It is up a hill, and that's where the wind comes in. When you feel the wind, I want you to start running for your life, and it won't be so hard to go uphill. Okay?"

"I'm ready." My wet hair and tear-stained cheeks felt like they needed some refreshment anyway. Colt closed his eyes and took my hand in his, but instead of jumping out of the truck, he paused.

"Lord almighty, please protect Hailey and me as we seek shelter in this storm."

"Amen," I replied. "Thank you for praying."

He nodded. "Let's go."

And with that, the door was open, with him helping me out and shutting it behind me. We were off, him holding my hand with all of his might and running me up the hillside. A giant gust came barreling towards us, and Colt was right; it made climbing a wet, muddy hill a little easier, until we both did a complete face plant, head to toe, in the mud. Colt got back up, pulling me up to his side like a rag doll. There was no time for it, and we both knew that, as our legs robotically kept fighting forward. After several minutes, we reached a flat area, and the barn was in sight.

"We're almost there!" He pulled me forward, our bodies almost completely mud free by the time we got there, again from the hard rain. When we reached the doors, he only then let go of my hand, using both of his to slide the barn door open. "Go!"

I ran into the small opening he had made, into the dark. There could be all sorts of creatures in there, and I would have never known it. As Colt shut the door behind him, he pulled out a flashlight.

The barn was huge—used as a shelter for equipment instead of animals, so while there were no haystacks, we could catch a few Z's. There was a big beautiful John Deere with a cozy warm cab and cushioned seats.

"Well," I said as I tried to regulate my heartbeat that was about as erratic as his windshield wipers. "That was something. Thank you for getting us to safety."

"Don't thank me yet. The storm isn't over."

I was weary at his notion that something bad could still happen to us there, but my feeling was that he was just being cautious. He found a few lanterns and lit each one, illuminating the whole barn, which made me feel even more safe. The rain pounded on the metal roof, and I yearned to be dry with a warm blanket on my couch, but this would have to do for the night.

"Thank you, Colt. I mean it." I turned to him, and he took a step towards me. He still had mud on his face, collecting in his laugh lines, eyebrows, and nostrils. As funny as the mud looked, it didn't even put a dent in his handsome looks. He reached up and put one of my wet curls behind my ear, his hand lingering on the gape of my neck. In my emotional state, I turned away, feeling down about the whole situation. "I'm sorry I've gotten you in this scenario." I felt tears coming again, but I choked them back.

"You don't have to apologize. I would have done the same thing. And I'd do it again for you, right now." He let go of my neck and looked up at the tractor. "Want to go sit in there? Looks a little more comfortable than standing around on this concrete floor."

"Yes, my feet are killing me. But how about this time, I push you into it by your butt?" reminding him how he helped me into his truck earlier. Though it was an entire emergency, and he did it as respectfully as he could, I needed to lighten the mood.

"You just couldn't let that one go, could you?"

"I haven't given you a hard time in hours. I'm starting to have withdrawals."

He looked at me sheepishly. "Forgive me if that was inappropriate."

"It didn't seem so at the time. It's all about context. If you did it now? You'd lose a hand."

He chuckled a warm laugh, bringing his sunshine demeanor back from stress. I managed to get into the tractor without his helping me from the bottom, but rather, he got in first and pulled me in beside him. It was nice and comfortable and being that high up meant we could see out a small window on the side of the barn. Colt's truck was in perfect view, and that far, had no harm done. But the truck bed was overflowing with water, and the river nearby was rising fast. Since we were protected by a steel barn, and inside another layer of steel in the tractor, the sound of the terrifying rain almost didn't seem real.

"I'm sorry about Cindy. I take it you were very close." I nodded, putting my hand on his from across the cab.

"Thank you. Yes, we were. I was closer to her than I was with Jett."

"Was?" And just like that, he called my bluff.

"Yes. We broke up almost immediately after I moved here." Colt stiffened in his seat.

"Why didn't you tell me?" His eyes were glaring, but his mouth was smiling; it was a brilliant combination of emotions.

"And what good would that do? Besides making my suffering public knowledge. Nancy would be setting me up with her nephews on a daily basis."

"She wouldn't have to. Because you'd be with me." Colt was as far away from me as he could get in the cab of the tractor, but with words like that, I needed more space.

"Not so fast, cowboy. No one ever said I liked you." I crossed my arms, turning my body to look straight ahead at a dark wall.

"Sure, you do. You pretend like you hate my guts, but I know what I know."

"Oh, right, Mr. 'I can see the future'?" I mimicked his voice a little too well, as if I'd been practicing. I hadn't, but it didn't look good for me.

"About that," he smiled, rubbing his hands together. "I suppose now I can tell you."

"Go for it. Make it the long version. I've got all the time in the world."

"Actually, never mind. You don't deserve it yet."

"Good. I didn't want to hear it anyway." A total bluff. There wasn't anything, besides the secrets of Ancient Babylonia that I wanted to hear more.

"Right."

Ugh. I could scream! That guy drove me crazy. "What is it about you that just makes my blood boil?" I asked him, point blank.

"I'd call it mutual attraction, finding your soulmate, predestination—"

I cut him off when I leaned in close to his face. I noticed the attraction, all right. His lips were mere inches away from mine. The electricity was off the charts—it felt like a livewire between us. I wanted to pull away—things were far too fresh for me to be thinking clearly, but at the same time, it was the clearest my mind had felt in months. Always the perfect gentleman, he waited for me to make the move. I started to lean in, just a little more, and saw his breath speed up. I could feel his chest rising with each breath from the weight of my arm. His face stood still, leaving me to land a kiss on his lips and-— I pulled away. "I'm sorry."

"Are you apologizing to me? Let's get this moment commemorated on a t-shirt." He played it sweet, which I appreciated.

"I just don't want this to go too far. We are in a confined space, alone, and uh—," I was about to give him the speech about why purity matters to me, but he took the lead.

"I don't either. I want to save all of this," he motioned to his face and body, "for my future wife."

I was surprised—and *elated*—to know that a man that gorgeous had the inner values to match.

"Yes, I totally agree. I do too. Save it for her." I smiled, putting my hands behind my head, trying to get comfortable. I let out a long breath of relief. Colt knew I was actually single, and had been from the moment we met, and it didn't turn into him putting the moves on me. He was a real gentleman. I turned my head to get a better look at him. He wasn't looking my way; instead, he was taking off his weathered cowboy hat and putting it on the dash of the tractor. He ran his tanned hands through his beautiful, thick hair, and he leaned over, untying his work boots, before slipping his feet out of them.

"You may want to do the same. Ever heard of trench foot?"

My mind sent me on a flashback to a frightening documentary about early shoe design. "Yikes, yes, I have. Aye, aye, captain." I struggled to slip out of my new rainboots for a few minutes before Colt offered to help.

"Here, toss your hogs up this way." Swinging my legs up in the air, I ended up hitting some sort of button on the tractor, causing a loud horn to go off. We both screamed in fright, causing us to go off in a tizzy of laughter.

We spent the rest of the evening talking. He told me all about his life; growing up in a small town and taking care of his siblings like a pseudo parent due to his father's failing mobility. Watching the strongest man he knew go through years of cancer treatments. Becoming an adult before he got to be a teenager.

"I'm only 25, but I've got lots of siblings, and I helped raise them all. My dad was sick nearly my whole life. He did everything he could to survive, but God wanted him sooner. But now, I live intentionally. We never know when our time is up, Hailey. And the most important thing is to honor God with our lives, our bodies, and our actions."

"I think I was supposed to meet you, Colt Wilder. You sure do tell me what I need to hear, especially when I don't want to hear it." I reflected for a moment. My controlling ways were not honoring God. My actions resulting from fear of loneliness were not honoring God. My resistance to losing the comfort in my life in exchange for the path He may have wanted me on was not honoring God. *So how do I break this pattern?* I shared my personal struggles with Colt, pouring my heart out with the soundtrack of the storm.

"One thing I noticed about you, right off the bat: You are your own woman, with big dreams. You don't let anything stand in your way. You came into this little pocket of Wyoming like a gale wind with all the lightning and thunder possible. And even though we don't have the same standards of perfectionism you were hoping for, I think you've blossomed in the realization that perfectionism and excellence are two different things, Hailey. You are what this town has needed all along. I see it, Big Horn News sees it, but I don't think you see how much you belong here. But I know how much you want to leave. So, I just ask before you make any decisions, you consider that the place God has placed you in might not be for a temporary blip in your career. Maybe this is it. Here. With me."

I smiled, listening to his words, but shook my head. "Look, I'm not disagreeing that God didn't plant me right here for a reason. I know He is working through my struggles with perfectionism and my control freak personality. But—," I paused, almost not wanting to say it, "I've worked really hard to get here. This dream has consumed my life since I was young. Would God give me these dreams if He didn't want me to explore them?"

Colt's eyes lit up. "Will you tell me about that, Hailey? How you decided on this career."

"My mother—she was a beauty like you'd never seen. She could have done anything in life if it wasn't for cancer. When she got sick, I was stuck to her like glue. One night, she gently shooed me out of the room, so she could take a phone call with an old friend and speak candidly. My entire body was pressed against the door, and I heard her say that if she could do it all over again, she would be a weather girl like Dana Summers. She died not too long after. And ever since, I couldn't let go of the dream. I had to become what she never had the chance to."

"But is it what you want, Hailey? Your mother sounds like a wonderful woman, who would have supported dreams of your own."

The lump in my throat reappeared. Talking about my mother, even fifteen years later, always made me feel emotional. "I get what you're saying, Colt, I do. And to answer your question: yes. I want this. Just on a much larger scale." I paused, relishing in the dream of the camera lights, big studios, and life-changing stories. "It sounds like you are just trying to convince me to stay here in this place that bores me to tears because you like me."

"I would be lying if I said I didn't want you to stay, Hailey. But just consider the fact that you are chasing these ambitions for the wrong reasons. I understand losing a parent; boy, I do. But God might have an entirely different plan for you, and you could at least consider that."

"Okay." My voice cracked. He had a point, although it was hard for me to swallow.

Colt relented, not giving me anymore trouble on the subject. The sky outside was getting darker, and Colt had a suggestion. "We should try and rest while we can. Tomorrow is going to be busy. Just the cleanup efforts alone will be overwhelming."

I agreed, and he leaned his head on his arm against the window. A few minutes later, I heard his breaths go softer and deeper.

The way he challenged me really ruffled my feathers. While I wasn't as annoyed as I usually was with him, my entire being felt like it was playing defense. Was there any truth to what he said? The more I considered it, the more I agreed with him. I was chasing ambitions and not God's will for my life. In fact, I was running from it. It was time I surrendered to Him completely. I spent the rest of the evening praying without ceasing, while Colt slept beside me.

Early the next morning, at the first light, Colt shook me awake. I awoke to my head on his shoulder; embarrassed that in my unconscious state, I crossed the seat boundary and used his shoulder for a pillow. He sat, snickering for a minute while I opened my eyes, listening for the rhythmic pellets of the rain. Instead, there was silence.

"Hailey." I checked to see if I drooled on his shoulder, but thankfully, my mouth was dry. "The rain stopped." Colt perched, looking out the window ahead of us. The wind was still whipping hard. He was right; the sky was clearing.

"What time is it?"

"Four thirty in the morning." Colt had his phone in his hand. "And there's more. Hailey. You're getting comments on the videos from all over the country." He handed me his phone so I could read them for myself. People were tagging news networks nationwide telling them to hire me.

"That's cute," I said, handing him his phone back. "I'm glad people enjoy our reports."

He tilted his head. "That's it? You're not elated to be going viral?"

I shrugged. "I mean, I don't know. I've never been online much. While I am aware of its magical powers to elevate people into positions, I'll have to just wait and see if it works for me before I get too excited." I felt the presence of my own phone in my raincoat pocket and assumed it was dead. Pulling it out to check, I had 3% battery remaining. "I suppose I could check my email. . .? Because you know, it's listed on our website. Someone could easily contact me."

Colt waited patiently, not saying a word while I clicked on the web icon and punched in my username and password for my work email. Nick had just set it up last week after he got tired of forwarding me tips people sent in on rogue animals being affected by the weather. My phone was old and slow, and we only had 1 bar of service out there in that steel barn, but eventually, my email loaded, bringing twenty-seven new messages along with it.

"Oh boy." I needed a cup of strong coffee before I could understand all of what I was seeing, but at first glance, I had email messages from nearly every larger network in the country. "Call me 'Ms. Popular'. I'm viral all right."

Colt smirked, but didn't smile.

"ABK News in Chicago wants to offer me a spot on their daytime news." I kept scrolling the messages. "And so does TBW, for their weekend rotation. Oh, here's a Sunday morning forecast offer from Go News Now." I kept scrolling, but there was one that made my heart drop. An unread message from *KA News* sat at the bottom of my inbox. The very station where Dana Summers was working. I gasped when I opened it, realizing it was a message from Dana herself.

"What is it?" Colt asked cautiously.

"Dana Summers wants to fly me out tomorrow to meet her. She has a junior position that she wants to speak to me about. I'd be working directly under her."

"Wow." Colt's jaw dropped.

This all felt like a dream. One I always wanted to achieve. But when it was actually at my fingertips, it didn't seem real. It didn't feel the way I'd always imagined it would. Though I realized that I had a chance at what I had always wanted, all I could think about was Jett. I wondered how he was holding up, and suddenly, I desperately wanted to talk to him. It was going to be a long day, and for some reason, I wasn't excited about it.

CHAPTER 10:
LOW VISIBILITY, HIGH STAKES

Between the storm cleanup, and grappling with grief from losing Cindy, it took me three days to reply to Dana Summers. But, within hours of my reply, I received an itinerary for my trip to meet Dana in Chicago. I printed it out at work, letting Nick know that I would be gone for two nights. He didn't seem surprised. "You've really put us on the map, Hailey. Of course, we will have you here as long as we can, but I know you've got great things in store for your life." *See, Colt?* I argued with him in my head. *Nick gets it.*

"Thank you, Nick. I have certainly enjoyed my time here in Big Horn."

Reflecting on the last several weeks, I felt a lump form in my throat as I clicked my beige high heels back into my office, where my pair of navy rain boots waited for me to change into before I went home. The puddles around the station parking lot were so massive, all they needed was a diving board and a lifeguard on duty, and I wasn't about to converse that in a heel. Those days, I could only be seen in heels while on air. I had gotten used to a little more casual lifestyle in Wyoming and felt comfortable in my skin. All of that would have had to change once I got to the city, and I knew it.

Once home, as I reviewed the details of my itinerary, I saw that I would arrive at six in the evening and would be spending the next two days at the studio and attending dinner with executives on the second night. I pulled out my suitcase and packed for the trip. I picked out a yellow pantsuit to wear with my white silk blouse, black pants to wear with my pink blazer, and the dress I wore at my college graduation that was inspired by Dana's own.

The next morning, I awoke early. My neighbors' rooster would be crowing any moment, and I savored the silence beforehand. Making a small pot of coffee as I readied for the day ahead, my thoughts once again turned to Jett. I didn't want to contact him that early, so instead, I prayed for him. Colt came to my thoughts soon after, and I talked to the Lord about my confusion on my feelings. Then, I prayed for my journey, and once again, relented to the Lord for His guidance on my life.

Slipping my Bible into my bucket bag, I drove to the airport forty minutes away.

Dana's team had booked me a regional flight out of Wyoming, and then a *first-class* ticket to Chicago. I had never flown anything but economy of course, so my mind was wandering to the luxuries that might await me as we loaded onto the plane. Heated towels? Foot massages? I sighed. Something about that whole thing just felt *off.* I shuffled down the corridor with my small roller bag and got in line to board the plane.

"Hailey?" My eyes widened at the familiar voice as I looked at him in disbelief.

"Jett?" What is he doing here? "What are you *doing here?"* My arms couldn't resist wrapping around his body, and he returned the hug.

"I could ask you the same question."

"Dana Summers wants to meet me." I shrugged, fighting off my emotions hard as seeing Jett made me feel the wound of losing Cindy all over again.

"Wow. That's incredible, Hailey. I'm so proud of you." He put his hand on my shoulder.

"Thank you, Jett. And you? Why are you flying to Chicago?"

"Clarity. I know it's crazy because you know, it's only been a few days. But I just want to go see the place. To be sure that I want to walk away from it. My dad's with me, too. He's just gone to get us coffee." My heart skipped a beat to see Bruce walking over, holding two paper cups.

"Hailey!" Bruce handed the coffee to Jett and leaned in for a deep hug. We discussed our trips, Bruce telling me how they were making an overnight stop in Denver to visit Cindy's sister, Jodie. Then, we discovered Jett and I were sitting next to each other on the flight out of Wyoming. Bruce smiled at the revelation.

"Bruce, I would be happy to switch seats with you so that you and Jett can sit together." Bruce shook his head.

"That's okay, Hailey. I haven't been on a plane in ages, and I want to see if they still make that magazine with all the goofy gadgets for sale. I'm in the market for a multi-purpose weed whacker that also cuts my hair." Jett was quiet while we talked, but didn't object to anything. "We will be sitting together on the next flight. You can waive at us from first class." We all chuckled and I felt awkward about my seat upgrade, but Bruce immediately sensed it. "I couldn't be more proud of you, Hailey. You deserve all the good that's coming to you."

After we took our seats, Jett and I started slowly conversing about his plans. "This is so weird, coming here right now. My mom went a lot sooner than I expected, but the school had said I could cancel my deferral if things had changed. And things have changed, because I've been living on this autopilot mode for the last few years. Trying to live up to the expectations that everyone around me had for me, without ever considering my own, or what God wanted for my life. And now, I don't know if I want to be who I have become." I put my hand on his while it sat on the armrest between us. "I don't know if I even know who I am."

"I know exactly what you mean, Jett. I'm struggling with the same questions."

"Really? But you've always known that you wanted to be a meteorologist. Like the very woman you're off to meet." His reference to Dana Summers made my heart sink. It was surreal to be there then, about to meet someone I very much admired since childhood.

"Truthfully, I don't know if it was my dream, or my mom's dream that I put on myself. Either way, I am happy with the work. I really do enjoy it. I just have to figure out on what scale." He nodded, and for the first time, we were both vulnerable at the same time.

As the plane took off and punched through the clouds, I felt my nerves peak as I gripped the armrests with white knuckles. Jett said little during our departure, closing his eyes as we burst through patches of rocky wind and stormy weather. It was the bumpiest take off I'd ever experienced, and I was in a state of constant prayer for smoother air.

As the plane evened out, I released my breath, sparking laughter between us. "I know. Flying in and out of the Rockies is quite the experience." We let off some steam as we joked about how awful it was, and our conversation naturally progressed.

"I know I've strung you along this summer, and for that, I'm sorry from the bottom of my heart." His eyes were sad.

"You don't have to apologize, Jett. You were going through a lot."

"Thank you, but that's not an excuse for my bad behavior. However, all this time has given me ample opportunity to consider my past and future. Hence this trip."

"For me, as well." Jett pondered my statement and paused. I felt a gentle nudge to speak about his mother, though it was raw to do so. "And there's something else I want to share with you. About your mom." I waited to see if the mention of his mother would be detrimental at this time, as the grief for all of us was still just so fresh, but he just smiled and looked hopeful. "When I spoke with her, before. That day you called me, before the storm?" I started rambling.

"I know, Hailey. Well, what did she say?"

"So many things; first, was that she was ready to meet Jesus." A warmth came over me thinking about her basking in God's glory. Jett looked burdened by grief, but he smiled through it. "Then she told me that she loved me like a daughter. That she saw my struggles and that love is a gift. And that sometimes, God sends people in different directions." Jett nodded, taking it in.

"That sounds like her."

"She didn't tell me to walk away from you. She told me to pray. To follow God's plan, even if it hurts. Even if it felt lonely, which is my biggest struggle. Boy, she could read me like a book." The silence between us lingered. I waited. Finally, Jett spoke.

"Mom told me something similar, a few days before she got really bad. Said she was proud of the man I was becoming, but she didn't want me to become someone just to make her proud. Told me to find my own calling." He turned to me fully at once, his eyes glassy but steady. "I think we both knew. . .You and I are holding on to something familiar.

Something good. But maybe not what God has planned for us." I nodded, a lump catching in my throat. "I'll always care about you, Hailey. Always." His voice cracked just slightly. "But I don't want to hold you back. And I don't think you're supposed to come with me on this next part of the journey." The tears flowed fully down my cheeks, drying as they came in contact with the curls touching my face.

"I think you're right," I said softly. A moment passed. Then another.

"I've been watching your weather reports," Jett said after a while. "You are incredible, Hailey. Whether or not you pursue big opportunities with Dana Summers, I want you to know that this town was made better because of you. And so am I." I looked beyond Jett, out the window. The clouds had parted below, revealing colorful fields stretching endlessly in every direction.

"I think God's shaking things up for both of us," I whispered. Jett gave a small, bittersweet smile. Being with Jett was *easy.* He was like warm milk, comforting, soothing and a gentle reprieve after a long day. Seeing him always made me feel like I'd just returned home. But I knew, he wouldn't be that person for me anymore.

"Let's not be afraid of the path we are on." Jett smiled as he spoke, fighting through his grief. And with that, we sat together in silence—not out of awkwardness, but reverence. For what was. For what would never be. And for what might still come. When we landed, Jett reached for my hand and gave it a gentle squeeze.

"Go get 'em," he said.

"You too," I replied, and meant it with all of my heart. As we walked into the terminal, I felt my heart leaning on the Lord for support. That may have been the hardest goodbye of them all.

"Have a good trip, Hailey." Jett gave me a short hug, as his dad caught up to us.

"It was great to see you, kiddo. Go make us proud, okay?" Bruce squeezed my arm lovingly, and I watched them walk away. Down the corridor, onto the flat escalator, and out of my life—at least, for that time. It wasn't goodbye forever, but it was a goodbye for the future we had planned.

Walking to my next flight, I stopped to get an iced latte. What coffee cannot fix, there may not be a cure for, as it stands. When I reached the gate, I sipped the vanilla drink and watched the news monitors. A clip of Dana Summers came over the screen, as she discussed a storm that was brewing in the

Northeast. My heart leapt when I saw her, but it wasn't out of excitement. I was nervous as could be. My thoughts turned to Colt, whom I hadn't seen or spoken to since the morning we woke up in the tractor. He stayed behind and helped cleanup efforts in the canyon, while Nick picked me up on the other side of the fallen tree and drove me home. I knew Colt was upset about my leaving, and frankly, it all moved a little too fast for my own comfort. *But this was everything I ever wanted. Right?*

I pulled out my phone, my finger hovering over his name. All I had to do was click on it, and I could speak to him. But he could do the same. Maybe he didn't want to speak to me? I put the phone away. My flight was about to board. I would pray about it on the way there and see if the night brought any more clarity.

The first-class experience felt like just that: luxurious. I may have been ruined from sitting in economy forever as they brought me my own personal water bottle instead of the little cup as I sat down. We also had our own flight attendant for just us four rows, which at first felt silly, but it was all she could do to keep up with the demands of the passengers. Champagne, coffee, and desserts were flowing freely. It was past noon, I supposed.

The flight dragged on, but I found earthly comforts in the pillow and blanket that was provided to me and watched a sappy movie about a lost dog. I normally swore off any kind of movie that involved pets, as I couldn't handle the emotions their characters brought, and I was already feeling keyed up. Terrible combination.

Before we landed, I went into the lavatory and got refreshed, using the little sink to wash up, brush my teeth, and redo my makeup. I felt like a new woman after I spritzed on a little body spray and a swipe of deodorant.

My itinerary said a black Lincoln Town Car would be waiting for me on the curb of the airport. I walked out with my roller bag in tow, smiling expectantly, and saw there was a sea of black Lincolns, as far as the eye could see. Then, I noticed the sound. The sheer volume of the honking made my head rattle. The voices of people yelling to hear over it made me dizzy. I could sense a migraine starting up almost instantly.

"Hailey Sinclair?" A driver in a black suit, complete with a cap and white gloves, walked up to me.

"Yes, that's me." His name tag read, "Francis."

"I thought so. Dana showed me your picture. She knows how overwhelming this port can be." Dana was right about that. Francis took my luggage, putting it in the trunk of his car. "Anything else you don't want to hold onto? I'm sending this to your hotel." It felt disorienting and *out of my control* to allow that, but I supposed in that world, it was normal. And I was reminded that God *was* giving me lots of opportunities to ease up on my control issues. I shook my head as I got into the backseat. I decided to just hold onto my large purse, extra heavy with my Bible in it. It was kind of perfect, actually, taking that with me, to serve as a constant reminder of who was really in control there.

When Francis started driving, he made conversation. "We're off to the studio now. You'll be met by Melissa, Dana's assistant extraordinaire, and she will show you the set while Dana finishes up her broadcast." His voice hinted at an accent.

"Thank you, Francis. So, where are you from?" I asked.

"Boston. You?"

"Long story short, Montana, then Oregon."

"Ah, so you're a true small-town girl at heart."

I had never considered myself a part of Montana, and my childhood was clouded by my mother's passing. But I wondered if there was more to my upbringing being in a small town than I realized. "Maybe. I guess. I'm not really sure where I want to be." My voice trailed off. Francis locked eyes with me in the rear-view mirror as we battled traffic. Bicyclists were weaving in and out around the cars. It was metal to metal, surrounded by high rise buildings and concrete.

"This is as good a place as any. I've been here for fifteen years now. And Dana? What a wonderful woman to work for. You couldn't ask for better." I nodded, looking out at a building that looked familiar. It looked like it touched the sky.

"What street is this?"

"Twelfth and Manor." I knew it. This was the very building I was supposed to have moved into after graduation. I analyzed the streets around it; it didn't feel like a great area. The sidewalks were littered with garbage and the building was in a bit of a shadow—and anything can happen in the shadows. As if he read my thoughts, Francis chimed in. "We will get out of this area soon. The studio is in a much safer place." Relief washed over me again. That building was not meant for me. *Thank you, Lord, for steering me elsewhere.*

When we finally arrived at the station, Francis shook my hand and promised he would take my luggage immediately to the hotel. I thanked him, and got swept away by Dana's assistant, Melissa, who peppered me with questions regarding my preference on coffee, food allergies, and shoe size.

"I'm an 8. Why do you ask?" I smiled, genuinely curious of what it had to do with anything.

"Our glam team will be reworking your style for your meeting with the executives tomorrow night. I'm guessing you're about a size four?" I nodded. Though it made me feel silly, I felt sad to not be wearing the clothes I brought with me. Before Wyoming, I would have been thrilled to be dressed. But a part of me was awfully used to wearing comfortable footwear and clothes that didn't cut off my circulation or require me to skip dessert every night. I looked down at my outfit; I had chosen to wear the pink blazer with black pants. It was feminine and elegant. Something that Dana would have chosen, I was sure of it.

We went to watch the last few minutes of Dana's segment on a tropical storm that was tracking in the Caribbean. Seeing her in person was like seeing your elementary school teacher at the grocery store—it was shocking. Since her place had always been on the television, I had to pinch myself to realize I was there, at the very studio that she made famous. When she finished her forecast, the camera turned off, and she was instantly surrounded by a flurry of producers, stylists, and lower-level assistants. Her flawless makeup was touched up with sponges, her nose gently powdered, and someone handed her a protein bar and a coffee—but she accepted neither.

"Is she here?" was all she could ask. I was there. She was speaking about me.

"Hailey is right here, Dana." Dana squinted through the lights, stepping off the podium and glamorously walking over to me.

"Hailey, so lovely to meet you. Dana Summers. I am so glad you are here." She reached out and shook my hand, her bracelet bangles clanging together.

"Wow, *the* Dana Summers. It's an honor to meet you. Thank you for having me." She did a coy curtsy and motioned to Melissa, who quickly pulled up the pen hanging from her clipboard.

"Order me a cold pressed juice, will you? Nothing sweet in it. And whatever Hailey wants." Melissa nodded, looking at me.

"I'll have what she's having. . .but sweeter."

"Hailey, let's go somewhere to talk. Melissa will bring us drinks." I followed Dana down a long, windy hallway. People stopped her constantly, asking for her opinions on fabrics, shoes, or hairstyles they wanted to try on her. She gave honest and sometimes brutal opinions to each one. Dana was definitely respected around there. It was fun to see it.

When we made it to her dressing room, it was as big as my rental in Wyoming, with a full lounge setup. It had floor to ceiling glass in the corner, overlooking the city. She motioned for me to have a seat in the lounge area, and she took a green overstuffed chair. I sat on the couch across from her, fighting the urge to kick off my heels. It had been a long day of travel .

"I'm glad you could make it, Hailey. I know you've been in a whirlwind after that storm. Speaking of, I've been watching your footage on repeat, and I love what I'm seeing." Dana winked as she beamed, using her hands to emphasize her words.

"Honestly, yes; this is a little surreal. The studio, the city." I shrugged, not wanting to sound ungrateful for the opportunity, but I was feeling quite overwhelmed with it all. "I've been watching you on television since I was a little girl. And now I'm here." Dana basked in the words.

"That is so sweet, Hailey. It was meant to be." She smiled lovingly towards me. Dana was as nice as I had hoped. But was it meant to be? "I was in your shoes once."

"You were?" I asked her, not believing she knew how much all of this was to walk into. It seemed more plausible that Dana was born into the world of glamour.

"Oh yes. When I was discovered by my agent, I was competing in a small-town beauty pageant at a mini mall. Not the most exciting thing in the world, if you can imagine. I was already in school, so when a news network took an interest in my 'image,' I changed my major from business to meteorology."

"I had no idea about that. And I've read all of your books." I smiled, feeling a little confused.

"The real nitty gritty never makes it on the page. I think most people just want to believe I was born into this. That I've always wanted to do this, like you. Not that I fell into it by accident." She smiled. "But I do see my younger self in you, Hailey. You've got the on-air charm that just can't be taught."

"Thank you, Dana. That means a lot coming from you." She nodded, waving at Melissa who walked in the door behind me, carrying drinks. Dana was silent as Melissa robotically set the drinks down on the table and quickly made an exit.

"I have a confession to make, Hailey." Dana took a sip of her bright, green juice, and I took a sip of mine. It was surprisingly good. "This isn't a meeting, as it is so much more than that. This is a proposal. You've got buzz, kid. The ratings for your little rinky dink studio in Wyoming don't lie—you've got that momentum that we want here at KA News. And there's a big wide career path here for you, if you want it. . ." That moment was the first time anyone assumed I might not want that for my life.

"What kind of career opportunities?" I asked.

"A guaranteed one. Given that you don't go viral for something royally opposite of your character, that is. But I know you aren't that type of girl. You are a good, smart woman who makes wise choices. And that's why I want you here. You'd be working under me. You would be my protégé." My jaw dropped. Dana laughed, clearly enjoying my reaction.

"You want to mentor. . .me?" I couldn't believe it.

"Yes, I really do. I want to pass on what I wish someone had done for me when I was your age. Back then, I thought the highest honor was to have a man choose me for marriage. Instead, I chose myself. And look at all the things I've gotten to do. While I never settled down with a partner, I've traveled the world and been the face of weather for two decades. I did it alone and so can you. All of this can be yours, if you want it." I looked down at her hands. She was wearing diamond rings on both hands. I had assumed she was married, though she never put those details in her books, which were more focused on her life as a weather reporter or behind the scenes of the network.

"The last thing I want to be is alone." I whispered the words, feeling sick to my stomach as they came out. Dana didn't miss a beat.

"I've chased this dream to the top. There is no one else at this level, Hailey. So, you've got to ask yourself: 'How far am I willing to go to chase my dreams?'"

"May I ask. . ." She looked at me and motioned for me to say it. "Do you ever feel lonely?" Her face went blank momentarily as she pondered a question I wasn't sure she was ever asked before.

"Sure, but I have everything I've ever wanted," she said with grit.

"Everything?"

"Everything except someone to pass on my knowledge to. That's where you can come in, Hailey." I saw then that while Dana was incredible for giving me that opportunity, she was yearning for connection, even if it was transactional.

"I'm not sure what to say, Dana."

"Just think about it. You have a bright future, Hailey. And together with me, it could be a bolt of lightning."

I left the meeting feeling shaken. Melissa called Francis to pick me up and told me to wait in the bottom floor lobby. As I pressed the button on the elevator, my hands could barely hold steady.

"Good meeting?" Francis asked, as he opened the car door for me.

"Yes. I think so. Thank you." The drive to the hotel was short, just a few blocks away, but more cars on a city block than the entire town of Big Horn parked at the Walmart on a Saturday night. From the outside, it looked like any other hotel in a city. Stone awning, doorman, with a plush carpet. But once I stepped into the double doors, I was in awe: sparkling chandeliers, oversized artwork in gilded frames, and an intoxicated scent being pumped out of the airwaves. A gentle piano could be heard nearby.

My room was no different; a grand fireplace, bright, crisp linens, and a view overlooking the sparkling city life. I couldn't kick off my shoes fast enough. Starving, I grabbed the room service menu and ordered a burger, fries, and a cinnamon roll, and while I waited, I opened my luggage and changed into some sweats. Taking up half of my suitcase was the pink teddy bear that Colt won for me at the fair. I didn't know why I brought it, but I held it close to my heart that night.

The food came quickly, and I dove in. I was halfway through the burger when another knock at the door came. It was the concierge, delivering me an outfit that Dana's studio had sent over. I hung it up on the back of the door, unzipping the bag. It was a muted beige dress with a blazer combo. The color did nothing for my features except make me look older. Maybe that was the point. A pair of matching slingbacks were inside as well.

I finished my meal, feeling gluttonous for ordering dessert on top of something so heavy, but I couldn't deal with my emotions. I felt like a basket case. "Lord, please help me. What is happening? What should I do?" I asked. Taking a bite of the cinnamon roll, I was disappointed at how stiff it was. You could tell it wasn't that fresh. It wasn't an individual recipe. It wasn't made with *love.*

I pulled out my phone and looked at my weather radar for Wyoming. It looked like another storm cell was passing through. My mind went to Colt. Was he okay? Had I hurt him? Were my feelings for him real? Did I actually love my job at the station? Was Carolina making those blueberry muffins with the white chocolate chips that she only made on Fridays?

As if I was struck by lightning, I realized I was homesick for Wyoming. Chicago was not it. I didn't know if it could have been, if things had been different. If I hadn't gone to Wyoming first. Hadn't worked for a little news station that had so little to report on, that it needed to take the weekends off just to recoup news.

If I hadn't met a man who made me want to scream. Colt was not the kind of guy I would ever have chosen to like. He said whatever came to mind, and it drove me insane. After several minutes, I worked up the courage to call him and see why he hadn't called me. To make matters worse, he didn't answer. Not only that, but his voicemail was full, and I didn't want to give him the pleasure of following up with a text that could make him think I liked him.

As I was pacing around the room, one hand holding my phone, the other, the stale cinnamon roll, I got increasingly worked up. Who did that guy think he was? How did he have such a hold on me? And had I really been in love with him from the moment I saw him? I let out a sigh that was more of a yell. *Yes.* And that scared me to death. Everyone I had ever loved had left me or died. Coming to terms with that fact was unnerving. But Colt—the man who was never anything but a beam of sunlight; the man I'd considered slapping for chewing gum too loudly—was the undeniably perfect match to my high-strung personality. He didn't let me get away with any of it. I hadn't given him an inch of grace, yet he'd given me nothing but.

Together, we were a team. He kept it fresh. And he was the most handsome man I'd ever laid eyes on.

It was clear to me all at once—my future was not in Chicago. I didn't need the view of city lights. I wanted to watch shooting stars in Big Horn, Wyoming. Live a quieter life. Know my neighbors. Have real relationships. For someone with a fear of loneliness who ran from anything real, you'd think this was the first place I'd go. But once t I was there, it was the last place I'd ever wanted to be.

CHAPTER 11:

FALLING FASTER THAN THE RAIN

I was already waiting at the bottom floor when Francis pulled up, and he looked at me with surprise, expecting to have the front desk ring for me to come down. "Good morning, Hailey. And how are you?" He smiled, but his eyes went to my outfit. I was wearing leggings, an oversized sweatshirt, and tennis shoes. My hair was a frizzy mess pulled back in a banana clip that looked like it was about to burst from holding too much hair. I didn't get much sleep the past night, and it showed.

"I was actually hoping you could take me to the airport." Francis closed his eyes and nodded, understanding.

"Of course," he said with stoicism in his voice. I pulled up the handle of my roller bag that I had been leaning on, and he loaded it in the trunk. We hardly said two words to each other on the long ride back through traffic to the airport. But when we arrived, I handed him an envelope.

"Can you give this to Dana for me?" He nodded, putting it in his jacket pocket. I had written her a letter of thanks; explaining what she had meant to me as a child, and how her career was an inspiration to my life. Then I rewrote it so I could have a copy for myself, for when I looked back on it in thirty years and couldn't recall what was said. Maybe I would regret it for the rest of my life. Maybe I would get back to Wyoming, and Colt would still be the biggest pain to my rear. But his unwavering smile had been the best part of my day since we met, and being away from it made me realize that.

Both flights were delayed, and all of the extra time to sit around had me feeling anxious. I decided to turn off my phone, for fear that a text would come in from someone, and I would have to explain my actions when I wasn't ready to face them myself. I pulled out my Bible instead, openly praying while reading that God continued to lead my path, even if it kept me in Big Horn for the rest of my life.

By the time I got back to Wyoming, a place I'd come to unconsciously refer to as "home," it was half past four. I went straight to the station, hair still a complete frizz ball mess, and dressed in sweatpants, looking for *him.*

Nancy was sitting at her desk in the front lobby when I walked in. While everyone knew I was to be gone for a few more days, she looked at me knowingly with a soft smile turning on her lips. Looking back to her computer, as my appearance was a disaster, she started typing.

"He's not here. Everyone is at the county fair, and I'm just finishing up mailing paychecks, then I'll be there, too. It is Saturday night, after all."

Instead of asking how it was that she knew who I was looking for, I just thanked her and ran back to the door. Knowing that everyone was dressed up western for the fair, I put my impatience aside and stopped by the rental. Thankfully, I had thought that one through: Last week, I had stopped in a western store and got a few things on a whim of hopeful spontaneity— another sign that I was really beginning to enjoy my life there. I put on a soft white sundress with a pink checkered button up over it and a pair of cowboy boots with little pink paisley designs embroidered on them. I also put on some makeup and curl cream in my hair. I looked as good as I could, with puffy, tired eyes, but my heart felt on fire.

On the drive over, I grappled with the idea that Colt could turn me down. I had been quite dismissive to his notions of my chasing dreams that weren't meant for me. Boy, was he right. I saw that finally. But I had to figure it out for myself.

After parking, I paid my admission to a woman in the booth and started my hunt for Colt. People were scattered everywhere, and in a town like that, it was a sea of cowboy hats. I couldn't find him anywhere, so instead, I decided I would let him find me at a place he was destined to show up.

"Ten rounds, please." I held out a twenty-dollar bill to the man running the shooting game. My first three rounds were complete misses. I held back my smile when I felt Colt's presence come up beside me. I peeked out the corner of my eye, and there he stood, arms crossed, focused on my aim. For the man who may very well have been the love of my life, he sure was holding back from his usual banter. A week before, he would have been giving me ten tips to Tuesday on how to better aim that rigged rifle. But not that day. There we stood, playing emotional chicken on who spoke first. On my last shot, I miraculously hit the right target and won a prize. I pointed to a yellow stuffed bear, the same style that Colt won for me the prior week. We still hadn't formally acknowledged each other, but I didn't toss away life in the big city to be evasive there with him.

"Colt: for you," I said, handing him the bear with both hands. He turned to me, arms still crossed, and his hat tipped ever so slightly.

"Why, thank you, ma'am." Usually being called ma'am would elicit feelings of being old or dated, but in that instance, much to my own chagrin—I found it charming. "Aren't you supposed to be off with the city slickers?" He looked down at the bear. "Or are you here to gather your things, and this is just something to remember you by?"

"You would know the answer to that if you answered your phone when I called." He put the bear under his arm, recrossing them.

"I considered it." He looked down at his boots.

"Oh yeah? So, why didn't you?" I asked, feeling anxious that I'd blown it with him after all.

"Because you have things you want to do in life, Hailey. Things I could never see myself a part of. I'm a Wyoming man true and through. I have a hard time being in Walmart on a Sunday after church service with the long lines and crowds. I couldn't survive in a big city, so I thought it best that I just didn't answer your call because I didn't want to hold you back."

"Well, as it turns out, God is holding me back." I smiled as he looked up at me.

"Really? Does this mean—," He uncrossed his arms, dropping the bear and putting his hands on my shoulders.

"Yes. Turns out, the big city life isn't for me. I met Dana, and she was lovely. Her life is just as glamorous as I thought. But her life? It just seems so incredibly lonely. All she has is her success, and. . .it's not the life I imagined in the end." I reached down to pick up the fallen yellow bear. "This place, though void of a frozen yogurt shop and a spin studio, has everything I want—and Lord help me, it has you, Colt Wilder. Even when I want to strangle you because you've focused on a rogue prairie dog in the background of my shot. Or when you set me up to get chased by a goat wearing a sweater."

"Filbert's video is breaking records on ViralVideo to this day," he laughed.

"And now, when instead of kissing me, you are making me come to you with this long-winded speech about how I knew I loved you from the moment I saw you and that made me afraid to the point of pushing you away—," with that, Colt pulled me close, and I closed my eyes, preparing for his kiss. But when he didn't lean in to plant his lips onto mine, I opened them back up. He was smiling at me in a soft, knowing way.

"Remember when you were gorging on one of Georgianna's cinnamon rolls, and I told you that I saw the future? I mean, I'm not sure if you did. You were pretty preoccupied."

"You remind me of this every chance you get. Of course I do. Now tell me what you meant."

"It was a God thing, Hailey. I saw you walk in that night. Well, actually I was facing the parking lot when your headlights about blinded me forever. But something about this erratic looking driver caught my attention." I softly punched his arm.

"I'm not erratic. It was a long day, and I was coming to terms with this being my home for at least a while. Be glad that's in the past."

"Oh, I am, I promise. Anyway, I see this woman walk in with hair larger than life, makeup all smeared like she'd been crying. My heart hurt for her, and I didn't even know it. She could have been crying about a triple homicide she'd just committed for all I knew. But there it was: clarity like I'd never had before. God told me, 'There she is, Colt. The woman you've been waiting for. Your future wife.' So, I prayed, 'God, if she is meant to be my wife, show me in all the ways that we will be together.' That's why I didn't chase you, Hailey. Why I wasn't clawing for your phone number or trying to kiss on you in the tractor. I knew that if God truly wanted us to be together, He would make it happen. And here you are, standing in front of me, when you're supposed to be heading up a weather segment on the national news as we speak."

My brain was on autocorrect. "Nah, I'd be fetching coffee for the people who do that." Then I pondered his words. "God really did bring us together, didn't He?" I looked around at all the people who lived in the town I would now call home. Smiles were found everywhere. The smell of funnel cakes ran thick through the air. Children holding brightly colored cotton candy with their sticky fingers. There was a joy in that town that I hadn't appreciated until I saw something else. When I looked back at Colt, he was holding my yellow scarf in his hand.

"I found this last night. Went out to the Duckweed Pond for some time with God. He is faithful to His promises. You standing here right now is proof of that," he pulled me closer, my head leaning on his shoulder.

"Are you going to kiss me now, or what?" I asked.

"Only if you'll ride the Ferris wheel with me." I gasped, taking the scarf from his hands and laughing, knowing full well I'd shared with him my fear of heights. "I promise; I'll protect you."

"What if they have to evacuate? What if the bucket with me inside spills out and I die? What if—," he put his fingers to my mouth, quieting my words and leaned in for an electrifying kiss as his pillowy lips molded into mine.

EPILOGUE:

FORECAST CALLS FOR FOREVER

1 Year Later

"Good evening, Big Horn Wyoming! This is Hailey Wilder reporting live from the Dunn Horse Pass Overlook. We've got several things happening tonight as a high-pressure system is moving westward, right into Big Horn. Enjoy this sunny weather while you can, because there is another storm on the horizon. Best to take out those winter jackets now and expect an early season snowfall for the foothills of Big Horn by Labor Day, because summer just put us on notice. Remember to give us a follow on ViralVideo at Big Horn News Network. Back to you, Donny." Colt cut the feed.

"Perfect, as usual, for my bride. But you forgot to include that there's a *100% chance for love*," Colt leaned in and gave me a peck on the lips.

"Should I promote you to script-writing? Because I think that would take a lot off my plate." Colt laughed, turning to his camera.

"Ready to go home?" he asked as he took his camera off the stand. "I think Bruno will be happy to see us. He hates that crate."

"He is such a good boy in the crate, because he can't get into mommy's shoes. But I'm starting to think we need to go back to the pound and get Bruno a sister. Maybe a playmate will do him well?" Colt laughed at the idea.

"I can't imagine two cute dogs demanding my pizza crust. I'd have nothing left to eat. Besides, I don't think Jett and Mandy will enjoy babysitting two dogs when we go visit your dad next month." The reminder of our upcoming trip made me feel excited.

"Yeah, you're right. We better wait until they get married before we get a second dog. Two high energy pups might cause some real chaos in their relationship," he said. I smiled thinking of how great it was that Colt's sister, Mandy, and Jett were together. They were the real soulmates for each other after all. With Jett deferring law school indefinitely while opting for insurance sales, and Mandy starting up her own Boba Tea cafe, they were a very busy couple as it was. Along with their wedding planning, we were lucky they agreed to take shifts with Bruno at all. Angie would keep him at her place overnight, while Bruno would have free roam of Jett's backyard during the day. It was a great setup, and we knew he would be spoiled while we were gone.

"There's something else, Colt." He turned, expectantly but with a look of surprise.

"What?"

I reached in my pocket and pulled out the ultrasound picture. "Lord willing, next March there will be a 100% chance of a baby Wilder." Colt's jaw dropped as I looked at him for his reaction.

"Seriously, Hailey? I'm going to be a father?" His eyes looked glassy as he took the ultrasound picture in his hand. Tears escaped his cheeks, and mine were soon to follow. My emotions were on overdrive that month, and that was how I knew why.

"Well? What do you think?"

He took me into his arms. "I couldn't be happier! This is everything I've ever wanted in life. Thank you, Hailey."

As we stood basking in the joy of our news, a rainbow appeared in the distance.

"God really changed the forecast when I met you, Colt."

ABOUT THE AUTHOR

Cassandra discovered her passion for writing at the age of seven when she purchased a diary at the Scholastic Book Fair. What began with journal entries about her school and home life later evolved into a collection of poems, short stories, and novels. Her hobbies include skiing, traveling around the Rocky Mountains, and reading. Much of her writing inspiration stems from her love of dogs, her Onondaga heritage, and her Christian faith. Cassandra's favorite genres of books are Christian fiction novels, Thrillers, and anything British.

She is a full-time writer and resides in the mountains of Wyoming with her husband, Chad.

cassandrajoelle.com

OTHER BOOKS

A New Leash on Life: A Dog-Mom Rom-Com, Book 1
Get ready for a hilarious Christian romantic comedy as we follow the journey of a thirty-something introverted woman, Katie Fitzgerald, who's longing for a husband. But when she accidentally adopts a dog, she discovers that love comes in unexpected ways, and that God's timing is always perfect.

Genre: Christian Romantic Comedy

Fetching Love: A Dog-Mom Rom-Com, Book 2
Three couples, three journeys, and one hilarious adventure on the unpredictable path to love. Katie and Eli are ready to say "I do," but the days leading up to the wedding are full of surprises- especially when Katie's mom's true crime sleuthing lands her in a pickle. Samantha and Mitchell seem perfect

together, but hidden struggles test their relationship. Can they find common ground, or will their opposing desires pull them apart? Carolyn and Micah have found faith and each other, but their surprise romance leads to a sudden, life-altering decision. As these couples follow the Lord, they find joy and laughter along the way.

Genre: Christian Romantic Comedy

The Après-Ski Proposal: A Romcom About Love Off-Piste
She came for a fresh start... Not a fake boyfriend. When Claire Riley gets dumped on the eve of her 30th birthday, she's blindsided. A spur-of-the-moment ski trip seems like the perfect escape, until she runs into her ex... With his new girlfriend. Shocked and desperate for a lifeline, Claire accepts a proposal from a charming stranger to pose as her fake-boyfriend. What begins as a simple act of saving face turns into a journey that reveals a fresh start in life and love—the kind that only God could have planned.

Genre: Christian Romantic Comedy

The Curse of Josephine Bagley
Over the course of a century, three individuals are woven together by a decades-old curse:

William, after surviving an Indian raid on his orphanage due to his facial disfigurement, goes on to live among the tribe. But when misfortune befalls them, he is quickly traded away and faced with a pivotal choice that changes his life forever.

Josephine has faced immense loss. Despite her granddaughter's efforts to help her find solace in faith, she finds she can't let go of the past and falls further into her belief that she's eternally bound to darkness.

Saraphina, a fledgling antiques dealer, gets the surprise of her life when a courier delivers notice that she's the last surviving relative of the Bagley Estate. What seemed like a windfall that could help her career now causes her to question her own reality.

In this tale of intertwining mystery, loss, and faith, these souls navigate through nefarious trials to find the gift of grace and forgiveness that extends to us all.

Genre: Christian Gothic